Nancy from

Grandma & Grandpa,

March 22, 1940

THEY RAISED THE POLES AND THERE WAS A TENT IN
PLACE.

Honey Bunch : Her First Days in Camp.   *Frontispiece—(Page* 78)

HONEY BUNCH:
HER FIRST DAYS IN CAMP

BY
HELEN LOUISE THORNDYKE
AUTHOR OF "HONEY BUNCH: JUST A LITTLE GIRL,"
"HONEY BUNCH: HER FIRST
LITTLE GARDEN," ETC.

NEW YORK
GROSSET & DUNLAP
PUBLISHERS

Made in the United States of America

CONTENTS

THE HONEY BUNCH BOOKS

BY HELEN LOUISE THORNDYKE

12mo. Cloth. Illustrated.

GROSSET & DUNLAP

Publishers   : :   New York

HONEY BUNCH:
HER FIRST DAYS IN CAMP

CHAPTER I

"THE PACKINGS"

"Now," said Honey Bunch importantly, "let me think."

Lady Clare, Honey Bunch's cat, comfortably stretched out on the lowest step of the back porch, blinked her eyes. Then she stretched out first one black front paw, then the other. After that she yawned.

"It's too hot to think," she seemed to say.

Of course, some people will tell you that cats can not talk, but Honey Bunch was sure they could. In fact, she knew Lady Clare could talk, for she had heard her. She "talked" when she wanted to come into the house and the screen door was shut, and she talked when she saw Honey Bunch coming up the garden walk, and, my goodness! how she talked when she was angry. Once Lady Clare had been angry at a new cat who had come to live across the street and such snarling and spitting you never heard! Honey Bunch could tell you that she heard Lady Clare cry, "Go away!" as plainly as any person could say it.

"I feel like thinking," Honey Bunch now told her cat. "I have lots to think about."

So she sat down beside Lady Clare and stroked her fur softly and began to think. Honey Bunch liked to think aloud, and that was fortunate for Lady Clare. She never had to ask questions.

"I'll tell you first, Lady Clare," decided Honey Bunch, "because I think you really ought to know it—you'll have to go and stay with Mrs. Miller, you see. I hope you don't mind?" she added anxiously.

Lady Clare blinked her eyes gravely. She knew she had been asked a question, but, as Mrs. Miller, the washerwoman, declared, you couldn't hurry Lady Clare; she took her time whether it was to lap a saucer of cream, or to come when she was called, or to reply when she was spoken to.

"Me-ow," said Lady Clare finally, and she began to purr gently.

"You don't mind, do you?" Honey Bunch cried joyfully. "I'll tell Mrs. Miller when she comes to-morrow. You liked it the last time you stayed with her—when we went to see the seashore. Remember?"

Lady Clare purred more loudly. She evidently remembered.

"Now this time," went on Honey Bunch's eager little voice, "this time, we're going to a camp—Mother and Daddy and I—we're all of us going. We're going to sleep in a tent. I never slept in a tent before, and neither did Norman Clark, nor Ida Camp, nor any of the boys and girls I know. You wouldn't like to sleep in a tent, Lady Clare, because you're a cat. But I think it will be fun. Daddy says perhaps I can go bathing, too. He says cats don't like water, but little girls do. Down at the seashore, Julie and I went in the water 'most every day."

Lady Clare's head had been going lower and lower and now the tip of her pink nose rested on the step. She was fast asleep.

Honey Bunch looked at her reproachfully —she didn't think it was polite to go to sleep when some one was talking to you. Still, Lady Clare might have been up all night guarding Mother's pantry lest the mischievous mice should come and eat some of the good things.

"If *I* had to stay awake all night and watch for mice, I'd be sleepy, too," whispered Honey Bunch. "No wonder you are tired, Lady Clare."

She crept away from the step very softly, so as not to waken the cat, and was creeping softly back with a red flower pot under her arm when some one called to her.

"Hey, Honey Bunch!" cried a gay voice. "Honey Bunch, what are you doing?"

A great noise and a tremendous shaking of the fence told Honey Bunch that Norman

Clark was climbing up on the other side.
Norman said that girls were no fun to play
with and that they liked silly games, but he
never failed to ask Honey Bunch half a dozen
times a day what she was doing or what she
was going to do. He often sat on the fence
for hours, watching her work in her garden.
He and Lady Clare were very fond of the
fence top. They could see what was going on
in the other yard, when they were perched up
there.

"What are you doing, Honey Bunch?" said
Norman again. "Where you going with the
flower pot?"

"I'm getting ready to go to camp," Honey
Bunch explained.

"Has the tent come yet? Can I see it?
Will your daddy put it up in the yard before
you go? Maybe he'll let me sleep in it? Say,
do you suppose he will let me sleep in it just
once?" asked Norman. "I'd like to sleep in
a tent, Honey Bunch."

Honey Bunch was used to Norman's questions. Mrs. Miller said he made her nervous,

he talked so fast, but Honey Bunch could always remember what Norman had said. He didn't make her nervous.

"The tent's down cellar," she answered patiently. "But it's all wrapped up, Norman. Daddy is going to leave it that way, to send on the train."

"Oh!" Norman said. "Well, perhaps I can sleep in it when you come back. How big a tent is it—as large as a circus tent?"

Honey Bunch didn't know.

"It must be big, if you all sleep in it," said Norman. "But I don't see what you want a flower pot for. What do you want a flower pot for, Honey Bunch?"

"I thought I'd take a plant with me," Honey Bunch replied. "To put on the window sill, you know. They may not have any garden, and my mother likes flowers in a house."

"There won't be any window sills," argued Norman. "Not in a tent. Don't you know how tents are? There is a door at each end, but not any window sills. There aren't any windows, so how could there be window sills?"

"Then I won't take the flower pot," Honey Bunch said wisely. "I'll leave it here. Lady Clare isn't going, either."

"Cats aren't any good in a camp," said Norman. "I'll bet Lady Clare would be scared if she saw a wildcat."

Honey Bunch, whose real name was Gertrude Marion Morton, was called "Honey Bunch," because, as her daddy said, she was so sweet. No one had ever seen her really cross. If she had been the kind of little girl who gets cross, she would have frowned at Norman now, for she didn't like to hear any one say that her dear cat was not brave. But Honey Bunch didn't frown—she only looked at Norman seriously and shook her head.

"Lady Clare wouldn't be afraid," she said earnestly.

"Well, she would if she saw a wildcat," persisted Norman. "Wildcats scare tame cats into fits."

"Then I'm glad Lady Clare isn't going,"

Honey Bunch said quickly. "I don't want her to be scared into fits."

"What's in the basket?" asked Norman, whose eyes had spied the clothes-basket under the tree. It was Mrs. Miller's "second best" basket, and she had loaned it to Honey Bunch.

"Those are my packings," Honey Bunch explained.

"Packings?" said Norman. "What are packings?"

There surely never was a boy who could ask more questions, or a little girl who would answer more patiently.

"Packings," explained Honey Bunch, "are the things you take with you when you go away."

"Well, what are you going to take with you when you go away?" Norman asked, banging his heels against the fence and delighting in the noise he made.

"Oh, lots of things," replied Honey Bunch. "I'm taking some of the shells I found at the seashore for dishes—did you know they cook things out of doors in a camp, Norman?"

"In shells?" Norman wanted to know.

"I think so," answered Honey Bunch. "Julie said they use shells at clam bakes on the beach, so they must in camp, too. And I have the sprinkler—I guess that will stand up in the trunk."

"What do you need a sprinkler for?" Norman asked.

Honey Bunch sighed a little. It seemed to her that Norman asked a great many questions. But then, she thought, he liked to hear about going to camp.

"It's for a shower bath, Norman," said Honey Bunch. "I asked Daddy, and there isn't any ocean at camp and Mother said they don't have bathrooms with tubs in them, either. So I can wear my bathing suit and Daddy will turn on the sprinkler, the way he does for us sometimes."

Norman was scrambling down from the fence, and he said something over his shoulder that Honey Bunch could not hear. Through a crack in the fence she saw him running into his house. In another minute he dashed out, carrying something that dragged on the ground behind him.

"Honey Bunch!" he gasped, climbing up the fence and making a worse racket than ever, because the something he held was bumping and clattering against the fence as he climbed. "Honey Bunch, here's something for you!"

He was red in the face as he pulled the "something" over and tumbled with it down into Honey Bunch's yard.

"What is it?" asked Honey Bunch, a little excited because Norman was. "What is it, Norman?"

"As soon as I thought of it, I thought you'd like it," Norman said proudly. "My father uses it in the automobile when we have company, but he won't care—you take it. If I go to camp next year, you can give it back and I'll use it."

Honey Bunch was still puzzled.

"What is it, Norman?" she said again.

"It's a camp chair!" Norman cried.

"A camp chair!" repeated Honey Bunch. "How lovely!"

She had seen the chair before—she remembered it when Norman opened it for her—but Mrs. Miller had called that kind a "folding chair." If a folding chair was a camp chair, why, of course, it must be just the thing to take to camp.

"I wish I had two more," Norman sighed; "one for your mother and one for your daddy. But perhaps you will not all want to sit down at once—you can take turns, you know."

"Thank you ever so much, Norman," said Honey Bunch gratefully. "I'll put it in the basket with my other things. I wish you could go to camp, too. I wonder what else I ought to take to camp?" she added.

"You want to take something to scare the wildcats," suggested Norman. "Are you afraid of wildcats, Honey Bunch?"

"I never saw any," Honey Bunch replied. "What do they do?"

"They go like this—" and Norman made such a terrible noise that he almost frightened himself.

CHAPTER II

IDA'S GIFT

HONEY BUNCH put her hands over her ears and Lady Clare sat up indignantly. Mrs. Morton, Honey Bunch's mother, came out on the back porch.

"What in the world was that noise?" she asked.

"That's the noise a wildcat makes," Norman informed her. "I was showing Honey Bunch."

Mrs. Morton laughed. She said she thought something had happened to Norman.

"Mother, look at the camp chair Norman gave me," said Honey Bunch. "It is to sit down on in camp, Mother."

"That is very kind of you, Norman," Mrs. Morton replied quickly. "But we'll not be able to take furniture with us, I am afraid.

We take our trunks, but the tents and the furniture are in a storehouse near the lake."

"But the tent is down cellar," urged Norman. "Honey Bunch said so. And she has a lot of things in the clothes-basket to take."

Mrs. Morton sat down on the top step of the porch and pulled Honey Bunch into her lap.

"What busy children you are!" she sighed. "That isn't a tent down cellar, Honey Bunch —it's a new grass rug for the porch. But we are not going to unroll it till we come home. And, my dear little girl, we can't carry all those things you have picked out. Besides, you won't need them in camp. What made you think you will want the sprinkler, dear?"

"For shower baths," explained Honey Bunch, "in my bathing suit, Mother."

"There is a whole beautiful lake of water waiting for you," Mrs. Morton said, smiling. "No, we'll leave the sprinkler at home. And now if you'll come in and decide which dolly you think deserves a trip to camp, I can go ahead with the packing."

Honey Bunch followed her mother into the house and Norman climbed down from the fence and went indoors to ask his own mother a question. Norman had just thought of something he wanted to do.

"I think I'd like to take my china doll to the lake," said Honey Bunch, when she had looked at all her dolls and told them about the camp and carefully explained that only one could go. "She has a bathing suit Aunt Norma knitted for her and the water never hurts her. It agrees with her."

The rest of that busy day, Honey Bunch trotted up and down stairs and helped her mother with the packing. When Daddy Morton telephoned in the late afternoon he asked to speak to his little daughter, and Honey Bunch, who loved telephoning, climbed up on the chair by the table to talk to him.

"I just wanted to warn you not to pack the cat," said Daddy Morton. "Mrs. Miller will take her to-morrow, you know."

"Oh, Daddy, I wasn't going to pack Lady Clare!" Honey Bunch assured him. "I never pack her. Mrs. Miller takes her in a basket, but that isn't packing."

"Well, I thought you might forget this time," answered Daddy Morton soberly. "I know how excited ladies get when they are packing. Anyway, I meant to ask you if you have the moth balls for Lady Clare."

"Moth balls, Daddy?" Honey Bunch repeated, rather puzzled. "What moth balls, Daddy?"

"For her fur coat and her ermine collar," replied Daddy Morton. "There is a large box of moth balls in this drug store where I am telephoning, and I happened to think that Lady Clare hasn't any for her fur coat. Shall I bring some home with me when I come to-night?"

"Mother," Honey Bunch called, "shall Daddy bring home moth balls to-night?"

"Moth balls?" said Mrs. Morton, exactly as Honey Bunch had done. "What in the world does he want with moth balls?"

"He says for Lady Clare's fur coat and her

ermine collar," Honey Bunch explained earnestly.

"You tell Daddy to stop teasing and not to forget to bring home the tags for the trunks," said Mrs. Morton. "He is teasing you, Honey Bunch."

Honey Bunch laughed, and at the other end Daddy Morton, who could hear what Honey Bunch's mother said, laughed, too.

"All right, I won't get moth balls," he announced. "But I'll go around to the ticket office and get our tickets—two whole ones, and a little, half ticket for you, Honey Bunch. That is all you need."

"Just half a ticket?" Honey Bunch asked, a little disappointed. "Why don't I need a whole ticket, Daddy dear?"

"I think it must be because you are only half as big as a person who takes a whole ticket," her daddy replied, and then Mrs. Morton came to the telephone and talked to him while Honey Bunch went outdoors to see if she could find some one to ask about this half-ticket matter.

"I know what a half ticket is," said Ida
Camp, who lived across the street from Honey
Bunch and was her very best friend. "They
cut a whole ticket in half and that is big
enough for children. If I were going with
you, I could have the other half; but I suppose
some other girl will use it now."

The first thing Honey Bunch said to her
daddy when he came home that night was:

"Where is half the ticket?"

"Half the ticket?" he laughed. "You seem
to think the ticket agent takes his scissors and
cuts a ticket in two pieces, dear. Here is your
half ticket. It doesn't look so very different
from mother's and mine, now does it?"

Honey Bunch said no; and indeed they all
looked alike.

"Ida Camp said some other little girl would
use the other half, Daddy," Honey Bunch said
curiously. "Will she?"

"Ida seems to be a little mixed in her ideas,"
answered Daddy Morton. "This is the way
it is, Honey Bunch, and you must tell Ida
when you see her: A half ticket merely means

half the fare—that we do not pay as much for
a little boy or girl as we do for a grown person. When you are twelve years old, you'll
need a ticket like mine, but until then you may
have what the railroads call a 'half ticket.'
Do you see, dear?"

"Yes, I know about it now," Honey Bunch
declared. "Perhaps Ida will like to see it—
the half ticket, I mean, Daddy."

And when Ida came over on the porch that
night after dinner, she saw the tickets and Mr.
Morton explained about them to her as he had
to Honey Bunch.

Mrs. Miller, the good-natured washerwoman, came the next morning and took Lady
Clare to her house to stay till the Mortons
came home again. Lady Clare was used to
visiting Mrs. Miller and Honey Bunch knew
she always had a pleasant time there. She was
waving good-by to the basket in which the
cat was—Honey Bunch said she knew Lady
Clare was peeping out between the wicker slats
and could see her—when Ida Camp called to
her to come over.

"Honey Bunch!" cried Ida. "Honey Bunch! Come on over! I have something I want to give you."

Honey Bunch ran across the street and up on Ida's porch. Ida looked excited.

"It is for you to take to camp," she whispered. "I made it for you," and she put something wrapped in tissue paper in Honey Bunch's hand.

Honey Bunch thought at first there was nothing in the paper that Ida handed her. It didn't weigh anything and it was so limp it folded up in her hand. But of course Ida wouldn't give her a paper with nothing in it; that is, unless she had made a mistake.

"I'll bet you can't guess what it is!" said Ida, bouncing up and down, she was so excited. "I made it all by myself."

Honey Bunch unrolled the tissue paper hastily. Out dropped a little green silk square. This was Ida's present.

"What—what is it?" Honey Bunch asked doubtfully. "A handkerchief?"

"It's a pillow cover!" Ida cried. "You put

pine needles in it. There will be pine needles where you camp, Honey Bunch, and you stuff the pillow with them. Then, when you come home, you have it in the parlor. My mother has one."

"Why, that's a lovely pillow cover, Ida!" said Honey Bunch, kissing her little chum. "I'll be sure to put pine needles in it and keep it in the parlor."

"I sewed it and I knew you'd like it," Ida declared, as she watched Honey Bunch go down the steps. "You're not going yet, are you, Honey Bunch? The girls said they wanted to say good-by to you."

"We're going to-morrow morning, early," explained Honey Bunch. "You tell Anna Martin and Kitty and Cora and the others that I'll come out to play this afternoon. I can see them then."

Honey Bunch went home to show her mother the pillow cover and to ask her how she put pine needles in it. Mrs. Morton laughed when Honey Bunch said that, but she said she thought Ida Camp was a dear little girl to take all that trouble to make Honey Bunch a gift.

"You must never tell her, dear, for you might hurt her feelings," kind Mrs. Morton said. "But I am afraid Ida forgot to leave an opening for the pine needles. She has sewed up all four sides of the cover, and one should be left open."

"Then isn't it any good?" asked Honey Bunch, much disappointed.

"Oh, of course it is a fine pillow cover, dear. See, Mother will rip the stiches on this end and we'll leave it open. You put the pine needles in here and I'll sew it up again for you, and when you come home you'll have a nice, fat little stuffed pillow to show Ida."

"Will you keep it in the parlor?" Honey Bunch urged, and Mrs. Morton said:

"Yes, indeed, the pine pillow shall go in the parlor."

CHAPTER III

A LOVELY SURPRISE

THE expressman came for the two trunks before luncheon, and he asked if Honey Bunch wouldn't like to go along.

"We can ship you by express, just as well as not," he said cheerfully. "You could sit on top of a trunk all the way. How would you like that?"

"I couldn't go," Honey Bunch told him. "Not now. I have half a ticket, so you see I must ride on the train."

"I'm always just too late," grumbled the expressman. "Well, if you are not going by express, I must hurry with the trunks. Perhaps they'll get to Tickaloc before you will."

That was the name of the lake where Honey Bunch and her daddy and mother were going —Lake Tickaloc. It was an odd name, wasn't it? Honey Bunch had to say it slowly or she found herself talking about "Lake Tick-tock."

Mrs. Morton and Honey Bunch had lunch together on the kitchen table—Honey Bunch dearly liked to eat a picnic lunch in the kitchen, and she thought it was much more interesting than eating in the dining-room—and then Honey Bunch went out to say good-by to the little girls she knew. She would not have time in the morning, for Daddy Morton had said they were to leave as soon as breakfast was over.

"Norman Clark says you're going to camp where there are wildcats, Honey Bunch," said Anna Martin, as soon as she saw Honey Bunch.

The girls were all cutting out paper dolls on Ida Camp's porch—Anna and Ida, Grace Winters, Kitty and Cora Williams and Mary and Fannie Graham. As they all lived on the same street and knew each other well, they were good friends.

"Will there be wildcats, Honey Bunch?" asked Cora Williams, staring a little fearfully at Honey Bunch.

"No, of course not, silly!" Grace Winters said quickly. "There might be wildcats in the woods, but they wouldn't be in camp. Norman Clark is always saying something like that. I don't believe a word that boy says."

"I do," said Honey Bunch, in her pleasant little voice. "Only I don't think there are wildcats at Lake Tick-tock—I mean, Ticka-loc. Daddy wouldn't let them hurt us, anyway."

"I wouldn't mind having a little wild kitten," Fannie Graham suggested.

"Now don't begin and ask Honey Bunch to bring things back with her," scolded Ida. "When she went to the seashore we all asked her to bring us shells and everything. My mother says Honey Bunch is so good-natured we don't give her any peace."

"You are nice, Honey Bunch," Kitty Williams said earnestly. "I won't ask you to bring me a single thing. Isn't that your daddy in his car? Perhaps he wants us to go riding with him."

The little girls dropped their paper dolls

and scissors and ran down to the curb. They
found that Mr. Morton did want them to take
a short drive with him.

"Be sure you come back to our house," Kitty
Williams said several times, and each time she
said that her sister, Cora, poked her with her
elbow.

When it was time to take them home, Mr.
Morton drove up to the Williams' house and
Kitty and Cora said that Honey Bunch must
come in "just a minute." The other girls followed, and what do you think?

There, in the porch swing, sat a wonderful
new doll, all dressed for traveling. She wore
a blue sailor suit and a red cape and a blue
hat with a red feather in it. She had a suitcase all her own, too, and a pocketbook with a
railroad ticket in it!

"Read the ticket!" Ida Camp urged. "My
brother Ned made it. Read the ticket, Honey
Bunch!"

It was lucky they knew what the ticket said,
for Honey Bunch was too excited to read.
Anyway, it always took her a long time and

her mother had to help, for she was only five years old.

"It says, 'From Barham to Lake Tickaloc,'" Ida said proudly.

Barham was the city where Honey Bunch lived, so it was plain that the doll was going camping with her.

"She is a present from all of us," Kitty Williams explained. "And her clothes come on and off!"

Dear me, so they did. There were buttonholes and buttons and hooks and eyes, just as there were on Honey Bunch's clothes. And there were more dresses in the suitcase, including a little suit of khaki, bloomers and blouse, just the kind of suit Honey Bunch herself had to wear.

"What are you going to call her?" Fannie Graham asked.

"Her name," said Honey Bunch calmly, "is Ida Grace Fannie Kitty Cora Anna Morton."

Though the little girls laughed, Honey Bunch insisted that was the new doll's name. She was always called "Ida Grace," but whenever strangers asked her name Honey Bunch would recite all six of the names.

Mrs. Morton had known about the doll, and when Honey Bunch brought Ida Grace home, after saying good-by to her little chums, she said that of course Ida Grace must go to camp with them.

"And Eleanor's feelings won't be hurt?" Honey Bunch asked anxiously.

Eleanor was her favorite doll, though she loved all her doll children dearly.

"Eleanor will understand that she hasn't any camp clothes," Mrs. Morton said comfortingly. "Now, Ida Grace is all ready to go —suitcase and all. You'd better introduce her to the china doll as soon as we get to the lake. Ida Grace has a bathing suit, I see, and they can go swimming together."

The Mortons were up bright and early the next morning after a good night's rest. Honey Bunch was so excited she was sure that she didn't want any breakfast.

"No one goes anywhere or does anything without breakfast," announced Daddy Morton, buttering a slice of toast for her. "Conductors and expressmen and the engineer who runs the train, all eat breakfast before they start the train. So of course the passengers must eat, too."

Honey Bunch did manage to eat her oatmeal and the toast and butter after that, but she had her hat on and Ida Grace in her arms long before the taxicab rumbled up to the door. The taxi man took the two bags out to the car first and then he delighted Honey Bunch by coming back to get the suitcase that belonged to Ida Grace. He was a very tall young chauffeur and Honey Bunch giggled when she saw him walking down the steps, carrying the little suitcase.

"That all the baggage?" he said smilingly.

"That's all," Mr. Morton answered, turning the key in the front door. "We are off at last, Honey Bunch!"

Down the street they rolled, past the houses where Kitty Williams and Anna Martin lived, around the corners of other streets, and down the shady avenue to the big railroad station.

Honey Bunch clung tightly to her mother's hand as they walked down the platform. Ida Grace smiled pleasantly—she liked traveling, that was clear. There were mountains of trunks on the platform—trunks that belonged to people who, like Honey Bunch, were going away.

"Is everybody going to Tick-tock, Mother?" Honey Bunch asked presently.

"Oh, no, darling—they are going to different places," replied Mrs. Morton. "Here comes a train for the seashore. You'll see some take that. If we wanted to, we could go to see Julie on that train."

Honey Bunch whispered to Ida Grace that she mustn't be frightened. The train made so much noise that it shook the station as it thundered down the track and stopped with a snort to take on passengers. There was a great scrambling and calling back and forth, some people got off the train and others climbed on, and then the engine puffed and groaned and began to move slowly again.

"Our train is directly behind this," said Mr.

Morton. "See down the track, Honey Bunch? It will be here as soon as this train is under way."

Sure enough, down the track was another panting and puffing engine. A man in blue uniform, wearing a white cap, began to walk up and down on the edge of the platform.

"Express for Mount Pleasant Way, Long Hills, Notch Junction and Lake Tickaloc!" he called loudly. "Cars ahead for Tickaloc! Take cars ahead for Tickaloc!"

Mr. Morton smiled at Honey Bunch and swung her up to his shoulder.

"We'll have to hurry," he said, picking up one of the bags. "It will be a long train, and we'll have to go pretty far forward."

Mrs. Morton took the other bag and they walked with a crowd of hurrying people far up the platform, almost to the end of the station. Fast as they walked, the train came more quickly and Honey Bunch was afraid, as the cars rumbled past them, that it was going right on and would not wait for them. But it stopped and the conductor and brakemen be-

gan to call out the names of the stations to
which the train was going, louder than ever.

"Lake Tickaloc!" they shouted. "Cars
ahead for Tickaloc!"

There were ladies with bundles and ladies
with bird cages and men with bags and bundles
and little boys and girls, all carrying something. Mr. Morton had Honey Bunch and a
bag and Mrs. Morton had the other bag and
her purse to carry and Honey Bunch had Ida
Grace and her suitcase. They were glad when
they came to a car and a porter in a white
jacket put down a little footstool and helped
them up the steps.

The car was pretty well filled with passengers and more kept crowding in. Daddy
Morton had a chair to himself and Honey
Bunch and her mother shared one together.
They were such comfortable seats, for they
could be turned around to face either the window or the aisle, and there was a little green
velvet cushion on the floor that was just the
thing for Ida Grace.

"And there's a cradle all ready for her, too," said Honey Bunch.

Several people heard her and looked curious.

"I don't see any cradle, Mother," a boy declared, as the train began to move out of the station. "Where is the cradle, Mother? Show me."

CHAPTER IV

GETTING ACQUAINTED

"Look, Mother," whispered Honey Bunch, forgetting about the cradle for Ida Grace. "Look, Mother, that boy is something like the one we saw on the train."

Mrs. Morton waited patiently. She knew Honey Bunch would explain.

"I mean the boy we saw on the train when we went to New York to see Aunt Julia and Bobby and Tess," Honey Bunch said. "The one who made faces, Mother, and spilled water on me."

Mrs. Morton remembered that boy. He had been on the train when she and Honey Bunch were traveling to New York. He had been such a disagreeable boy that it wasn't easy to forget him. He had made faces at Honey Bunch, and, oh, dear, he didn't act nice at all, even when Honey Bunch found he lived in the same apartment house with her cousins. His name was Lester Morris.

"I don't believe this boy is like Lester, do you, Mother?" whispered Honey Bunch. "He looks nicer."

The boy wasn't making faces. In fact he was smiling. He stood in the aisle, holding on to his mother's chair by one hand to steady himself.

"Where's the cradle?" he asked, looking directly at Honey Bunch.

"Up there," the little girl replied, pointing to a brass basket that was hung between the windows. "That's a cradle."

"People put their hats and coats in those," said the boy earnestly. "And bundles and things like that."

"But Ida Grace could sleep in it," Honey Bunch declared.

The boy's mother smiled at Mrs. Morton and said something to her son in a low voice.

"I'll put your doll up there for you," the boy offered. "Of course it can be a cradle,

if you want to call it one. Are you going
to Lake Tickaloc?"

Honey Bunch nodded and handed Ida
Grace to him. Somehow, she did not feel
afraid lest he play a trick on her. This boy
had a kind and merry face and such truthful
brown eyes that Honey Bunch liked him at
once.

"We're all going to Lake Tickaloc," said
the boy, as he stood on the edge of Mrs. Morton's chair and Mr. Morton held on to him
by one arm so that he could not fall. "Everybody in this car. There, I guess your doll is
asleep already."

"We'll be neighbors." The boy's mother
smiled and Honey Bunch saw that she had
brown eyes exactly like her son's. "My name
is Mrs. Francis Evans, and this is Francis,
Junior, but we call him Frankie."

Mr. Evans was sitting across the aisle, and
he got up and shook hands with Honey
Bunch's daddy. The two mothers went right
to talking and Frankie told Honey Bunch
about the other people in the car that he knew.

"We went up to camp last year and so did those folks down at the end of the car," he told her. "I don't like that boy much. His name is Saunders Abbott and he takes everything away from kids younger than he is. I don't know the people in the next two chairs, but that girl with red hair is my cousin Jennie Kirk. Her two sisters are coming next week. There'll be more children up at the lake when we get there. Some of them go in July and stay all summer. We live in Chester. Where do you live?"

Honey Bunch said they lived in Barham, and she told Frankie all about *her* cousins, Bobby and Tess and Stub and Julie and about Lady Clare and Norman Clark and Ida Camp and all the other little girls she knew. They were talking so eagerly that the train stopped at another station and went on, and they never knew it. But suddenly they heard something they had not heard before.

"My goodness, listen to that baby cry!" said Frankie Evans. "I guess he doesn't want to go to Lake Tickaloc."

The baby was a new passenger. His mother and he had got on the train at the station just passed and it was plain that something about the trip did not please him.

Honey Bunch peeped around her mother's shoulder and saw the baby, purple in the face and screaming so loudly that the old lady who sat next to him had her hands over her ears.

"Guess I'll have to go make faces for him," said Frankie seriously.

"Oh, don't make faces!" Honey Bunch begged. "Lester Morris does that. I think it is mean to make faces! And, besides, you'll scare the baby."

"Huh, I have to make faces at home to stop my sister's baby from crying," boasted Frankie. "Babies like to see me make faces. Just you watch."

Frankie went up quite close to the baby and put his fingers in his mouth—in his own mouth, of course, not the baby's. Then he shut one eye and pulled down the corners of his mouth. The baby stopped crying and stared and the other children began to laugh.

Honey Bunch laughed, too. Frankie did look funny.

"What are you laughing at?" said Frankie, shaking a finger at the baby. "You shouldn't laugh at me."

Then he let the corners of his mouth go *up* and he opened the closed eye and shut the other one and pulled down his nose. Honey Bunch didn't see how he could do it, but he did. The baby chuckled.

"Well, I never saw a trick like that," the baby's mother said gratefully. "Once Charles Augustus gets to screaming, he usually keeps it up for hours and hours. You're a very good boy to come over and stop him."

"Are you going to Lake Tickaloc?" asked Frankie.

"Yes, my aunt has a camp there and we're going to visit her," the baby's mother replied, a little surprised.

"We're going, too. Our camp is Camp Chester, and any time you can't stop the baby from crying, you send for me and I'll stop him," promised Frankie. "I don't mind making faces for him any time."

"You're very kind, and I may send for you," the baby's mother answered politely. "My aunt's camp is at the south end of the lake—Camp Cozy, she calls it. I'm Mrs. Hendricks, and the baby——"

"You told me—he's Charles Augustus," said Frankie, who seldom forgot a thing any one told him. "All right, Mrs. Hendricks, any time you want him to stop crying, all you have to do is to tell me."

Mr. Morton, who had overheard—indeed nearly every one in the car could hear—laughed a little.

"I'm afraid Frankie is undertaking a large contract," he said to Mr. Evans. "Suppose Charles Augustus starts crying at midnight?"

"Ten babies crying at midnight wouldn't wake up Frankie," Mr. Evans declared. "When he goes to bed he sleeps till morning, so we'll hope the crying is all done in the day time."

"I think those were funny faces," said

Honey Bunch, when Frankie came back and sat down beside her on the floor again.

They liked to sit on the floor, for, as Honey Bunch explained to her mother, "it didn't tilt."

"You weren't afraid, were you?" Frankie asked her. "I didn't look like Lester Morris, did I?"

"My, no, not a bit!" said Honey Bunch quickly. "I like to watch you when you are making faces. No wonder Charles Augustus laughed."

The other children in the car—and there were several, including Jennie Kirk, Frankie's red-haired cousin, and Saunders Abbott— came up to ask Frankie to make more faces now. He was most obliging and made one after another till he explained his face was tired.

"What can we do?" asked Jennie, when Frankie refused to make another face. "There's nothing to do. I wish I had brought my doll."

"I have a doll," Honey Bunch said.

"Would you like to see her? She is asleep, but I guess she has had a long enough nap."

There were two other little girls besides Jennie. Their names were Dora Green and Jessie Waller. They, too, said they would like to see Ida Grace very much. So Frankie climbed up on the chair and brought the doll down.

"Let's go across the aisle and play with her," Jessie Waller suggested. "There's an empty chair there. No one will take it now, because the train doesn't stop any more till it gets to the Junction, and then it only drops off some cars."

Jessie had been up to the lake before and she knew just what the train did each time.

Every one in the car was busy talking to some one else. Since they were all bound for Lake Tickaloc and would spend several weeks together, they were getting acquainted as quickly as possible. Mrs. Morton said Honey Bunch might go across the aisle, if she would remember to play quietly and not disturb older people.

"What a cunning suitcase!" cried Dora Green, when Honey Bunch showed them the little suitcase and the pretty clothes packed in it.

"And see the pocketbook!" Jennie Kirk said. "With a ticket in it, too, just like a real ticket."

"Here's the conductor!" announced Frankie suddenly. "You'd better give him that ticket, Honey Bunch."

The tall conductor laughed as Honey Bunch held up the little ticket for him to see, but he punched it gravely, just as he had the real tickets, and handed it back to her.

"The young lady doesn't have to change cars. She goes through to the end of the line," he said, and went on.

Honey Bunch folded up the ticket carefully and put it back in Ida Grace's purse. Then she turned to speak to Ida Grace and gasped. The doll was gone!

CHAPTER V

IN THE STAGE COACH

"WHERE'S Ida Grace?" asked Honey Bunch, much worried. "Who picked her up? Where is she?"

No one knew. All had been watching the conductor punch the ticket. But Frankie Evans thought he understood what had happened.

"What did you do with that doll, Saunders Abbott?" he demanded crossly.

"What would I do with a doll?" Saunders retorted. "I don't play with girl's stuff, do I?"

"You'd think it was funny to tease Honey Bunch, though," scolded Frankie. "You'd better hand that doll back if you have it, or I'll tell the conductor."

Saunders make a face at Frankie. Not a nice face—it reminded Honey Bunch of the

faces Lester Morris had made at her on the
train to New York.

"Let's look on the floor. Perhaps she fell
down," Honey Bunch suggested. "Don't be
cross, Frankie. Maybe we'll find Ida Grace
if we look."

She didn't want Frankie and Saunders to
quarrel, and she didn't believe that Saunders
had taken Ida Grace. Surely, he wouldn't try
to tease her when he hardly knew her!

The children got down on their hands and
knees to look, Saunders among them. Then
the old lady who was in the chair next to the
one where no one sat and where the children
had been playing, suddenly leaned over and
pulled something from under the back of
Saunders' blouse.

"Isn't this the doll you're looking for?" she
said calmly.

Saunders Abbott had slipped Ida Grace into
his blouse when no one was looking, just to
bother poor Honey Bunch.

"Didn't I tell you?" whispered Frankie, as
the train began to slow down for the Junction.

"Didn't I tell you? He always does something like that!"

It was some time later that Mrs. Morton called:

"The next station is ours, dear. Come and get your hat on, Honey Bunch."

"I see the stage!" shouted Frankie, a few minutes later. "Look, Mother! Look, Honey Bunch! There's the stage! I hope I can ride up in front! Say, Mother, do you suppose I can ride up in front?"

Honey Bunch could not see out of the windows on the side where the station was, for there were too many people in the aisle.

"Don't forget Ida Grace," said Mr. Morton, as they waited for the train to stop.

"Have you the doll's suitcase, dear?" Mrs. Morton asked, as the train stopped and still they had to wait because not every one could leave the car at once.

"See the stage, Honey Bunch?" buzzed Frankie, who would have galloped over the seats if he could, he was so eager to get to the door.

Honey Bunch held tightly to Ida Grace and her suitcase. She tried her best to see the station and the stage, but she was so little and every one else was so tall that she could not see a thing. She wondered what a stage was and if she, too, might "ride up in front." That sounded exciting.

"Where's the stage?" said Honey Bunch, as she jumped from the top step into the tall conductor's arms.

He was standing on the platform and he had seen her coming, so he caught her safely.

"There's the stage, right over there," he told her. "Going to help Jenks drive?"

Honey Bunch thought the station was a pretty place, as indeed it was. It looked like a log cabin. It was built of brown logs and there were red flowers growing in window boxes. There was a long platform with no roof over it and one end of this was piled high with trunks. It seemed to Honey Bunch that every one on their train had been going to Lake Tickaloc, the platform was so crowded. Every one was laughing and talking at once and a man who sat on a high seat in a queer-looking carriage was shouting very loudly and very slowly.

"This way for the camp!" he kept saying. "This way for Lake Tickaloc! Stage leaves in ten minutes. Get your seats for Lake Tickaloc."

"Shall we take the stage?" asked Mr. Morton. "There are other carriages, Edith, if you think you won't be comfortable."

"Oh, the stage will please Honey Bunch," Mrs. Morton said quickly. "I suppose it will shake us up dreadfully, but we can stand that. You never rode in a stage, did you, Honey Bunch?"

"Is that one?" said Honey Bunch, staring at the funny carriage and the driver who was still shouting. "Oh, yes, Mother, let's ride in the stage!"

Mr. Morton laughed and said that settled it and they must hurry and get their places. There was a railing around the top of the stage, and the suitcases and bags and satchels were piled up there, out of every one's way.

But Honey Bunch said she would rather carry the suitcase that belonged to Ida Grace, and when the driver saw it he said, yes, he thought that was a good plan.

"Once I lost a lady's suitcase for her. It fell off and tumbled down the side of the hill," he explained. "I've always been mighty careful since that not to run any risks."

Honey Bunch clung more tightly than ever to the doll's suitcase. She certainly did not want that tumbling down the side of the hill.

"Sure you didn't ever lose any passengers, Jack?" asked Mr. Evans, his eyes twinkling. "Never spilled any down the hill, I suppose?"

"No, sir, I never did and I never aim to," the driver answered. "Everybody in? Well, Billy and Tilly, I guess we might as well be going."

He clucked to his horses and the stage started so suddenly that Honey Bunch almost fell out of her seat.

"Hold on to me, dear," her mother whispered, smiling. "We're going over a bad road and there will be a good many bumps."

The stage was crowded with passengers, and
each time it struck a rut some one was sure to
bounce out of his seat. It was very funny to
see them, and every one laughed. No one
minded that until Saunders Abbott slid down
to the floor as the stage lurched around a sharp
turn in the road.

"Don't you dare laugh at me!" Saunders
shouted crossly as Frankie giggled. "I'll
punch you, that's what I'll do!" And he tried
to reach across Honey Bunch, who was sitting
between her mother and Frankie.

Mr. Morton took Saunders by the arm, and,
my goodness, you should have heard Saunders
roar! Why, he made so much noise that even
the driver heard him above the clatter of the
horses' hoofs and the creaking of the wheels.

"Hey!" he called out, in amazement, peer-
ing through the little window behind the high
seat where he sat to drive. "What's all this?"

"You might as well let him be, Mr.—er—
whatever your name is," Saunders' mother
said, looking anxiously at her son. "He will
scream as long as you try to stop him."

"You let me punch that Frankie Evans!"
cried Saunders, struggling to free himself.

He began to kick, and his sturdy shoes hit
Honey Bunch on one ankle and hurt her so
much that the tears came into her eyes.

"Say, I don't have any ructions like this in
my stage," the driver announced, as much as
to say that he didn't know what was allowed in
other stages where Saunders might have trav-
eled. "Anybody that gets so plumb wild he
kicks a girl has to get right out and walk."

"Oh, Saunders, be a good boy, won't you?"
Mrs. Abbott implored. "Don't make a scene,
dearie."

And all the reply Saunders made to this was
to open his mouth and shriek. He was so
angry, you see, that he couldn't even talk.

"Whoa!" said the driver loudly, and the
horses stopped.

"Now young man, you get out and walk
till you feel more pleasant," directed the stage
driver firmly. "You won't get lost, because
you can follow us. But I don't aim to have all
these folks made uncomfortable just because

you have a kink in your temper. Out you go!"

Saunders stopped crying. He stared. Frankie stared, too, and so did Honey Bunch. The driver seemed to be in earnest. Would he really make Saunders climb out and walk?

"I—I don't want to walk!" the bad boy stammered. "It's hot. Mother, do I have to get out and walk?"

"I don't care what you do," his mother told him wearily. "Ever since we started, you've acted like all possessed. Perhaps if you have to mind some one you'll be easier to live with."

Now, Honey Bunch didn't like Saunders— how could she? He had made faces at Frankie and hidden Honey Bunch's doll and kicked her on the ankle. But here was his own mother saying that she didn't care what he did! And Saunders looked as though he had expected his mother would care very much!

"Please don't let him get out and walk," said Honey Bunch eagerly. "He isn't crying now. Are you, Saunders?"

"No, I'm not crying now," Saunders repeated.

"Well, perhaps you've stopped for good. But I don't know," the driver said. "Can you smile? Let's see you smile!"

Saunders managed a grin. It was not a very gay smile, but still a pleasanter expression than he had worn for several minutes.

"This time you needn't get out and walk," decided the driver. "But don't let me hear any more of these performances. Hold fast now, folks—we have to make up for lost time."

He chirped to the horses, and, with a great creaking and groaning, the stage moved forward. Saunders snuggled down beside his mother and kept as still as a little mouse. Every now and then he glanced up fearfully at the driver's broad back—he wasn't quite sure that he wouldn't turn around and say he had changed his mind.

The road had been full of ruts and Mr. Morton had counted thirty-one jolts, to Honey Bunch's intense interest, but now they began to climb a steeper grade.

Up and up went the stage and the good
horses bent their heads and pulled steadily.
They never stopped for breath, but when they
reached the top of the grade and the driver
called "Whoa!" they seemed to be very glad to
rest. They stood quietly, their sleek coats
dripping with perspiration, and they were
breathing so fast that you could, Honey Bunch
said, "see them breathe."

"Going to rest the team a minute and let you
look at the view," said the driver, climbing
down from his high seat.

"Come, Honey Bunch, I'll take you out and
we'll see if our bones are still in the right
places," said Daddy Morton.

"Take Frankie, too, Daddy," Honey Bunch
suggested. "And Saunders—please, Daddy."

Both boys were glad to get out of the stage,
and they did exactly as Mr. Morton told them
to do.

"Frankie, take hold of my hand and,
Saunders, take hold of Frankie's," said Mr.
Morton, giving his other hand to Honey

Bunch. "Now, then, this is as near the edge as we'll go."

The road was narrow, and they stood between the stage and the "jumping off spot," as the driver called the precipice. As far as you could look, were mountains and valleys and, in one direction, a shining something that sparkled in the sun.

"That's the lake," said Mr. Morton. "Lake Tickaloc, where you and the china doll are going bathing, Honey Bunch."

Honey Bunch smiled and pressed a little closer to her daddy. She felt like a very, very little girl in a very big world.

"How would you like to go coasting down this place in the winter, Honey Bunch?" the driver asked.

He was tightening up the harness and seeing that the brakes were "all set" for the rest of the way, he explained.

"I wouldn't like it," replied Honey Bunch, a little shyly. "I might ride into a tree."

"Well, yes, that's true," the driver admitted. "I guess, come to think of it, only the fairies

go coasting here, anyway. They have magic
sleds."

Honey Bunch wanted to ask him more
about that, but he was climbing back into his
place and it was time to start.

"By the way," said Mrs. Evans, as the stage
began to go downhill, "what is the name of
your camp?"

Honey Bunch had not thought about names.
She had always said, "We're going to camp."
Even when Frankie told her about Camp
Chester and Mrs. Hendricks had said her
aunt's camp was named "Camp Cozy,"
Honey Bunch had not paid a great deal of
attention.

Mrs. Morton was looking at Honey Bunch
and smiling now.

"The name is a secret, for a little while, I
believe," she said. "But as soon as we are
settled, every one will know it."

CHAPTER VI

LAKE TICKALOC

THE horses were trotting along briskly now, for they were going downhill. The stage bumped and rattled as much as ever, but at least it was easier for the patient beasts who were pulling such a heavy load.

"Weren't you ever here before?" asked Frankie, watching Honey Bunch straighten the hat on Ida Grace.

Every time Honey Bunch looked at Ida Grace, that doll's hat was over one eye!

"No, I wasn't ever here before and my mother wasn't ever here before and my daddy wasn't ever here before," Honey Bunch said in a sing-song little voice.

"Why, yes they were, too," said Frankie. "Your daddy told my daddy that they were. I guess you were too little to remember it."

Honey Bunch looked troubled. She didn't

like to say that Frankie didn't know what he
was talking about, but of course he was mistaken. She *knew* that she had never been to
Lake Tickaloc in all her life, and of course if
her daddy or mother had ever been there, she
would have heard about that.

"I'll ask Daddy by and by," said Honey
Bunch to herself. "When he isn't talking to
Mr. Evans."

Rattlety-bump-bang down the road went
the stage. It flew over a little wooden bridge
that sounded as though it were going to ex-
plode like a cannon (but it didn't—Honey
Bunch looked back and it was all right) and
presently Frankie gave a delighted shout.

"There's the lake!" he cried. "Gee, some
of the boats are out! See the flags! Say,
Mother, the Winner camp is open. Mother,
they have their flag up. Oh, Mother, do you
suppose Joe Winner brought his canoe?"

Immediately all the children in the stage
were as excited as Frankie. They stood up
and peered at the lake, and if the doors had
not been tightly fastened I am afraid some of

them would have tumbled right down the steps into the road. Mr. Morton held on to Honey Bunch, for he said he didn't wish her to fly out of the window.

"And here you are!" cried the driver, swinging the stage around sharply and bringing it to a stop before a long, one-story house painted a bright yellow. "All out for Tickaloc House!"

Every one climbed slowly down from the stage, for they were a little stiff from sitting so long in one position and Saunders Abbott's foot had gone to sleep so that Mr. Morton had to carry him down the steps. Honey Bunch looked about her curiously.

She saw a little group of buildings, built in line with the yellow building. The yellow building was the hotel, she learned later. The general store and the post-office and the town garage were in these other buildings.

Across the road was the lake, a broad, smooth sheet of water on which several boats were floating. The land curved around the lake and there were tents and bungalows set

back from the water. Little wharves were
built out from these camps, and, as Honey
Bunch watched, a launch puffed out from one
of these and went chugging across the lake.

"Doesn't that breeze feel good!" said Mrs.
Morton. "Well, Honey Bunch, here we are
and our fun begins right away."

Honey Bunch held up Ida Grace to see the
lake. She wondered about the china doll who
had been packed in the trunk.

"David, have the trunks come?" asked Mrs.
Morton, when her husband came up with the
bags he had taken from the top of the stage.
They had not fallen off and Honey Bunch was
relieved when she saw them.

"They'll be over at the bungalow," Mr.
Morton replied. "Are you ready? The
launch is leaving in a few minutes."

"You could stay with us, just as well as not,"
said Mrs. Evans, who had overheard. "Our
camp has been open a week—my sister and
her husband came up early—and you wouldn't
be a bit of trouble."

Then Mrs. Morton explained that they had

telegraphed to the woman who owned a bungalow and that she would be expecting them.

So they went down to the wharf where a little white boat was waiting and Honey Bunch shut her eyes while her daddy lifted her in. She rather expected to find herself in the water, but when she opened her eyes there she was on a hard red velvet seat and next to her was Mrs. Hendricks with the baby.

"Did he cry?" asked Honey Bunch, instantly forgetting that she had been worried about landing in the water.

"He's been asleep, and I do hope he stays that way till we get to Camp Cozy," Mrs. Hendricks said. "You went in the stage, didn't you? Did you enjoy the ride?"

Honey Bunch said yes, and then more people climbed into the boat and in a few minutes they had started.

"Here we are!" Mr. Morton said, almost before Honey Bunch had time to see where they were going.

She blinked her eyes and her mother laughed.

"You and I can walk to the post-office and back every day, can't we, dear?" she said. "But Daddy thought we must be tired from our trip, so he wanted us to take the boat. Besides, we had the bags to carry."

They had stopped at a wharf painted white, and now Honey Bunch followed her daddy and her mother up this and found herself at the steps of the cunningest bungalow she had ever seen. It was painted white and it had green window boxes and green shutters with little white acorns painted on them. Honey Bunch had never seen a white acorn, but she thought they looked very pretty on the shutters. There was a little sign over the porch of this bungalow and on it were the words, "Acorn House."

"Is—is it a camp?" asked Honey Bunch doubtfully.

"Not our camp, dearest. We are going to have a tent," her mother explained. "We'll

stay here to-night. Are you hungry, Honey
Bunch?"

And just as Mother said that a little lady
with white hair opened the door of the
bungalow and darted out to greet them. She
wore a green dress, and what do you suppose
she said?

"Aren't you starved? I have fried chicken
for dinner and it's done to a turn!"

Honey Bunch thought she must have heard
what her mother had said, and the idea of
fried chicken "done to a turn" made the little
girl's mouth water. Honey Bunch had been
so busy making new friends on her journey
and seeing new sights that she had not paid
much attention to food. But now she remembered that it must be far past the regular
lunch time and that she had had nothing but
one red apple since her early breakfast.

"How do you do, Mrs. Applegate?" said
Mrs. Morton, shaking hands with the little
white-haired lady. "You look just the same.
Here is my little girl, Honey Bunch, you
know."

"Oh, I know all about you, Honey Bunch," Mrs. Applegate declared, kissing her. "Indeed I do. Now, you just go in that first door and take your hats off and I'll have dinner on the table when you come out."

There was cool water in the pink pitcher on the washstand in the quaint little room Mrs. Applegate had set aside for them, and Honey Bunch was glad to have her face and hands gently sponged. Then she brushed her hair herself, while her mother hunted for a clean handkerchief and her daddy opened the bags for them. Then they went out to the dining room and ate that fried chicken!

"You see, dear, we'll stay here to-night, and to-morrow Daddy will put up the tent and we'll begin to camp," Mrs. Morton explained. "It takes time to put up a tent and to see about the furnishings, and Mrs. Applegate wanted us to spend the night with her because she was so eager to see you."

"I knew your daddy and mother the first time they were ever at Lake Tickaloc," said Mrs. Applegate, nodding and smiling as she cut a square of sponge cake for Honey Bunch and filled her glass with milk the second time.

Honey Bunch almost choked on her cake. Frankie had said something like that, too. And she was just as *sure* that this was the first time Mother and Daddy had ever seen the lake.

"I think I'll lie down in this comfortable hammock and rest," Mrs. Morton said, when they had finished dinner and she had helped Mrs. Applegate with the dishes in spite of her protests. "Honey Bunch, don't you want to take a nap?"

Honey Bunch wasn't a bit tired and she was far too excited to sleep. She wanted to see all there was to see and to go wherever her daddy was going. She knew he was going somewhere, because he was looking at a paper in his hand.

"I thought I'd walk over to the storehouse and see about the things we'll need," he announced. "If Honey Bunch isn't sleepy, let her go with me and you'll have a nice rest, Edith."

This was lovely, and Honey Bunch skipped
along beside her daddy like a gay little rabbit
—indeed she hopped just the way you have
seen rabbits hop when they are out taking a
walk.

"Daddy," said Honey Bunch suddenly,
"were you ever at Lake Tickaloc before?
Frankie thinks you were, but I know he isn't
right."

"Why, dear, of course I've been here before, and so has Mother," Mr. Morton answered, in surprise. "I thought you knew,
Honey Bunch. Haven't I ever told you?"

"No, you never, never did," answered
Honey Bunch, shaking her head.

"Mother and I came to Lake Tickaloc the
year we were married. That was before you
came to live with us, you see, and that's the
reason we came this year," explained Daddy.
"So you would be acquainted with the lake,
too."

"Oh!" said Honey Bunch. "Oh! And did
you know Mrs. Evans and Frankie and Mrs.
Hendricks, Daddy?"

"No indeed. None of those people were here then," her daddy answered. "Mrs. Applegate was. Mother and I boarded with her. But there were no camps or other bungalows built then. It was very quiet and peaceful, and in a way I am sorry it is getting to be such a summer resort."

"But it is nice to have Frankie and Jessie Kirk here and Mrs. Hendricks and her baby," said Honey Bunch seriously. "And Saunders Abbott can be nice, maybe, when he wants to be nice. I like to have other children to play with, Daddy."

"So you do. And I am glad I have a sociable little daughter," Mr. Morton declared, lifting her over a barred gate which they had reached. "It would be rather lonesome, I suspect, for one little girl. Now, Honey Bunch, here is where we get our stuff for the camp."

Honey Bunch saw a building set behind the barred gate, a building which seemed to be made of sheets of tin and to be too small to hold all the things it was expected to hold.

Some of them were bursting out of the windows, in fact, and others had already tumbled out and were lying about the yard.

"Hello, Mr. Morton," said a tall young man standing in the doorway. "I thought you were coming to-day. Got the flag you ordered and the tent and everything. Pretty, isn't it?"

He was holding out a flag, a blue flag with white letters on it. Honey Bunch could not tell what it said.

CHAPTER VII

CAMP SNAPDRAGON

HONEY BUNCH stared at the flag, her blue
eyes puzzled.

"That flies from our flag pole, under the
Stars and Stripes, Honey Bunch," her daddy
explained. "It will tell people the name of
our camp."

"Mother said it was a secret," said Honey
Bunch.

"Well, and so it was. But now is the time
to tell the secret," declared Mr. Morton, taking the flag. "Look, dear—tell Daddy what
this spells: S-N-A-P-D-R-A-G-O-N."

Honey Bunch knew. Of course she did!
She couldn't spell very well herself, but she
had an excellent memory and she had seen
those letters often enough in the flower cata-
logues and heard them spelled out by Norman
Clark who, when he read aloud, had a great

habit of spelling most of the words he came to.

"Snapdragon!" cried Honey Bunch. "Oh, Daddy, it's Snapdragon—like my flowers, Daddy."

"For your flowers," Mr. Morton told her, smiling. "The camp is named for your prize flowers, Honey Bunch."

"I wondered about that name," said the young man, who had brought out the flag.

Then Mr. Morton told him about the prize flowers Honey Bunch had raised in her garden and which had won the grand prize at the annual flower show in Barham. And the young man, whose name was Larry Bert, said that his mother was "crazy about flowers" and that she had a garden and Honey Bunch must come and see her flowers as soon as she had time.

"I suppose you want to see about your stuff," said Larry. "Don't let the little girl fall over anything."

Honey Bunch didn't intend to fall over anything, but when she found herself inside the storehouse with her daddy, she began to think

that it wasn't going to be very easy to keep
from stumbling. You never saw such a place
as that storehouse was!

Honey Bunch thought what fun she and
Stub and Julie could have playing hide-and-
go-seek around the tables and under the chairs.
There were dishes on the tables and dishes on
the chairs, lamps sitting on the floor between
the rolled-up rugs and cots tucked away in
every corner and on these cots everything in
the world from books to frying pans and alarm
clocks and washbowls and pitchers.

"It looks a little messy, perhaps," Larry
apologized, as he helped Honey Bunch over a
pile of boards. "But, as I tell Mother, I know
where everything is. If some one came in
here and cleaned the place up, I wouldn't be
able to find a thing for a week!"

Mr. Morton laughed and asked where the
tents were. They happened to be behind a
pile of oil stoves, and Larry—who was certainly an obliging person—cheerfully moved
five stoves to get at them. Mr. Morton se-

lected the one he wanted and asked when the carpenters would put up the floor.

"Jed was fixing on coming to-morrow, right after breakfast," Larry answered. "I saw him last night and he promised to come over. If that is your list, you'd better let me have it and I'll gather up all the things you want and put it together. Then, first thing in the morning, I'll bring it out to your camp."

Mr. Morton said he thought that would be a fine plan, and he gave Larry the list and he and Honey Bunch scrambled over a table and crawled around a cot or two and found themselves outdoors again.

Honey Bunch and her daddy walked back to the bungalow by way of the lake and they stopped twice, once to see who could throw a stone and hit a rock that stuck up in the center of the lake and once to listen to a bird that was singing somewhere close at hand. They could neither one of them hit the rock and they couldn't discover the bird, but Honey Bunch said to never mind—perhaps next time. That was what Mrs. Miller said when she was disappointed and found she had put too much starch in some of the clean clothes.

You may believe that Honey Bunch was glad to go to bed early that night. In fact, she was so sleepy that she could not keep her eyes open through supper. She kept blinking at Mrs. Applegate and eating baked apple, until, finally, down dropped the spoon and Honey Bunch was fast asleep.

In the morning she woke up first and pattered over to the window. The green shutters were fastened back, and from her room Honey Bunch could see the beautiful lake already shining in the sun.

"I could climb over the window sill," said Honey Bunch aloud.

The window was so close to the ground that she could have stepped down into the soft grass by taking out the screen.

"Better wait till you're dressed, though," said Daddy Morton's voice. "I might want you to help me with the tent, and the carpenters would think you were a little ghost."

Honey Bunch laughed, and she and Daddy

had a pillow fight until Mrs. Morton said that
any one who wanted breakfast that morning
must begin *instantly* to get ready.

"For this," said Mrs. Morton, tickling
Honey Bunch, who was laughing at her from
behind a pillow, "is going to be a busy day for
the Morton family."

Mrs. Applegate was bustling around the
kitchen when Honey Bunch went to ask her
for a drink of water.

"I have cantaloupe and batter cakes for
breakfast," said Mrs. Applegate. "With
maple syrup," she added.

Honey Bunch found afterward that whenever Mrs. Applegate saw any one, she was sure
to tell them what she was planning to have to
eat. Mrs. Applegate was never happier than
when she was cooking something.

"I have a pie and a layer cake for you to
take over to camp, when your tent is up," she
told Mrs. Morton that morning, at the breakfast table. "Of course you won't be able to do
much cooking till you are settled."

As soon as she had eaten her batter cakes—

and, oh my, they were good!—Honey Bunch
trotted out after her daddy, who said he was
going over to see whether the carpenters had
come.

"That is where our camp will be, Honey
Bunch," said Mr. Morton, pointing to a small
clump of pretty white birch trees. "We'll
have a view of the lake from our front door."

There was a horse and wagon tied to one
tree and two men in blue overalls were lifting
out a pile of clean, white boards.

"Are they going to build a house, Daddy?"
asked Honey Bunch. "I told Norman we
were going to live in a tent."

"So we are, dear, but the tent must have a
floor," her daddy answered. "The carpenters will build us a nice, tight wooden floor
and then the ants and other little bugs will not
insist on helping us keep house, especially in
the sugar bowl."

"Do ants like sugar?" Honey Bunch demanded, and her daddy said that ants were
very fond of sugar.

The carpenters said "good morning," but

they seemed to be too busy to talk much. They were measuring the boards and some heavy timbers and marking them and presently they began to nail them together.

"If we didn't have to have a floor we could have a raft and go sailing on the Lake," said Mr. Morton, and one of the carpenters laughed and replied that a raft was all right in fair weather, but a rowboat was safer most of the time.

"Larry Bert said to tell you he is sending your stuff over and he'll haul the trunks from Mrs. Applegate's, too," the carpenter man declared, smiling at Honey Bunch as he spoke and tossing her a white, curly shaving from the board he was planing to make it smooth.

It was very interesting to watch the carpenters building a floor for the tent. They seemed to know just what to do. Honey Bunch was afraid they would hit their fingers instead of the nails, but they didn't. Every time, the hammer came down squarely on the nail head. And neither carpenter swallowed a nail,

though Honey Bunch looked the other way
each time they put nails into their mouths.

"My mother doesn't let me put things in my
mouth," she said at last, when she saw one of
the men take five nails at once and hold them
in his mouth.

"That's right—you mustn't do that until you
are grown up," the carpenter replied earnestly.
"I have a little girl, and I don't let her put
things in her mouth, either."

"Of course it is different when you are
grown up," said Honey Bunch, feeling better
at once.

It didn't take the two carpenters very long
to finish the floor, and before they had it done
Larry Bert had driven up with the things
from his storehouse. He was whistling and
he brought a dahlia for Honey Bunch. He
said his mother had sent it to her.

"I'll lend a hand with the tent, if you want
me to," he offered, and Mr. Morton said he
would be very glad indeed to have him help.

Honey Bunch looked on excitedly as they
unrolled the dark brown canvas. She meant

to see just how a tent was put up and then, when she went home, she could explain it to Norman Clark. He was sure to ask her a hundred questions.

"I don't see where the pole is," said Honey Bunch to herself.

She was sure that every tent had to have a pole to hold it up. Hadn't her Uncle Peter drawn her pictures of Indians and their tents and didn't a pole always go through the center and a neat little tent around this? And wasn't there always a flag on top? Why, of course that was the way. Honey Bunch had often drawn the flag herself.

"Pole?" said one of the carpenters when she asked him. "Bless you, we have 'em—three poles. Just you watch."

So Honey Bunch watched. The carpenters spread out the brown canvas and they took three poles and fixed them just as Honey Bunch did when she made a tooth-pick house —one pole at each end and a long one across the top. Then with Larry and her daddy helping, they raised the poles and the canvas

up and just as Honey Bunch thought it was
all tangled up, there was a tent in place.

"We're short two pegs," said Larry.

"I'll whittle a couple," Mr. Morton offered,
smiling at Honey Bunch, who was wondering
what the "pegs" could be for.

She saw in a minute. There were six stout
strings on each side of the tent and these were
tied to strong pieces of wood hammered into
the ground. They held the canvas and kept it
from blowing.

"That's green wood," said one of the carpenters, taking the pegs Mr. Morton had
whittled from a piece of stick he had found
on the ground. "If there's a storm, they'll
snap."

"Oh, we won't have a bad storm—not in the
summer," said Honey Bunch's daddy. "Want
to come in and look around, Honey Bunch?"

Honey Bunch did, and she stepped inside
the tent. It wasn't dark, for the tent was open
at either end and that let in plenty of light.
It was as large as their parlor and dining room

at home, and Honey Bunch thought it very comfortable indeed.

Mrs. Morton and Mrs. Applegate came as soon as the tent was finished, and then Larry said he would bring in the cots and set up the stove. There were three cots, canvas ones, and three low chairs—Mrs. Norton said the trunks would serve as seats, too, when they had company—and a table painted white. Larry carried in two wide boards with hooks screwed into them, and Honey Bunch was puzzled to guess what they could be.

"Wait till I get the kitchen put to rights and the bathhouses built and then I'll show you," Larry promised.

"Are you going to build some more?" asked Honey Bunch, dancing along beside him as he went back to the wagon. "Are you going to build some more? Let me watch you build the bathhouses, please, Larry!"

CHAPTER VIII

PAYING CALLS

LARRY had a mischievous twinkle in his eyes.

"Sure, I'll let you watch me," he said. "Shall I fix the kitchen first or do the building?"

"I wish you'd do the kitchen, if you don't mind, Larry," Mrs. Morton said, smiling at him.

She was down on her knees unpacking dishes and pans from a barrel and Mrs. Applegate was helping her.

Larry said he would fix the kitchen "that minute," and he took another roll of brown canvas from his wagon.

"I'd do anything your mother asked me to do," he said to Honey Bunch. "When she smiles at folks like that she just makes you want to do something for her."

"Yes, she does," agreed Honey Bunch. "Mrs. Miller says she has a way with her."

Larry laughed and asked who Mrs. Miller was.

"You have a way yourself," he told Honey Bunch, when he had heard. "There, that's a pretty neat kitchen, if I do say it myself."

While he had been listening to Honey Bunch tell about Mrs. Miller, Larry had been winding the brown canvas around three stakes he had driven into the ground, near the tent.

"Where's the kitchen?" asked Honey Bunch, in surprise.

"This is it," Larry said, pointing to the canvas. "That's all you need—something to keep the wind off when you're cooking. Now I'll get the stove."

There was a two-burner oil stove in the wagon, and as he put this on two large smooth stones and made sure that it rested straight, Larry explained that a stone fireplace went with each camp, but that a "kitchen" like this was of more use than the fireplaces.

"It's all right to cook your supper over an

open fire and have parties and things like
that," said Larry. "But when it comes to
cooking three meals a day, you want a fire you
can depend on."

"Now you build the bathhouses, don't you?"
Honey Bunch suggested.

She had been waiting patiently for this.

"Yes, now it's time to build the bathhouses,"
said Larry, and he took another roll of canvas from his wagon.

And, would you believe it, all the "building" he did was to wind the canvas around
three trees that stood together in one place
and around two trees that were close together
in another place.

"They're really outdoor dressing rooms,"
said Larry, smiling. "No one needs bathhouses when camping right on the lake; but
mothers have found that some one is dressing
or undressing fifty times a day in the tents
unless some kind of place is fixed up for the
kids; so I invented this plan. The trees make
good poles, now, don't they?"

Honey Bunch said yes, they did, and when

her mother called to her to come and get the china doll, she forgot to be disappointed. She was very glad to see the china doll again and she introduced her to Ida Grace at once.

"Want to know what the boards are for?" Larry called to her.

Honey Bunch was most curious to know what the boards with hooks in them were for, and she watched Larry closely as he screwed them tightly to the cross beams of the tent frame. He put one in one corner and one in another.

"Now that may not look like a closet to you, but it is," he told Honey Bunch. "There's a cretonne curtain goes over it and you hang your dresses on the hooks, and there you are!"

Honey Bunch said "Oh!" Camping, it was easy to see, was going to be great fun.

By noon Camp Snapdragon was really quite comfortably settled. The two flags were flying from the flag pole—each camping site had a flag pole—and the teakettle was singing cozily in the canvas "kitchen."

"I just brought you over a few things, because I knew you'd be too busy to do much cooking to-day," said Mrs. Applegate, coming in with a large basket.

She had slipped across to the bungalow and she had brought the Mortons—in addition to the pie and cake she had said she had made for them—bread and cookies and jelly and a roast chicken. Mrs. Morton declared that she wouldn't have to cook for a week.

"Wait till Honey Bunch and her daddy get their camp appetites," said Mrs. Applegate wisely. "This air makes folks hungry."

Honey Bunch was counting the seeds on top of a caraway cookie when a whistle sounded outside. The carpenters and Larry had gone home before the noon hour, so it could not be their whistle.

"Honey Bunch!" called a voice. "Say, Honey Bunch, are you around?"

"It's Frankie—Frankie Evans!" Honey Bunch cried happily. "Isn't it, Mother?"

It was Frankie, and he put his head inside the tent door and smiled at them.

"My mother sent you some plums, Mrs.

Morton," he said politely, holding out a basket. "Say, your camp looks great with the
flags up. Have you been in swimming yet?"

Mrs. Morton took the plums and asked
Frankie to thank his mother for them.
Frankie said he had had his lunch when he
was asked to sit down, but he did take a cookie
and seemed to like it.

"I thought perhaps Honey Bunch would
like to take a little walk and get acquainted
with the other children," he explained.

"Oh, yes, Mother, I'd like to take a walk!"
Honey Bunch said eagerly.

"Then don't stay too long and do not try to
walk too far, dear," Mrs. Morton answered.
"And no swimming, Frankie—not till she
goes in with Daddy to-morrow."

"All right—we won't even paddle in the
lake," Frankie promised. "And she won't
have to walk far, Mrs. Morton. All the kids
live right around here."

Honey Bunch started out with Frankie, and
the first camp he showed her was where he

and his mother and father were staying, Camp Chester.

"We've had it every year for six years," he said. "I'm eight. How old are you, Honey Bunch?"

"I'm five," Honey Bunch told him. "How old are Jennie and Saunders?"

"Jennie is almost seven," replied Frankie, picking up a stone and "skipping" it into the water. "And I think Saunders is nine. That is his camp, over there."

Honey Bunch looked and saw Saunders Abbott on the porch of one of the bungalows.

"Gee, now I suppose he'll want to come with us," Frankie sighed. "I didn't know he was at home—he goes to the post-office about this time every afternoon."

Sure enough, Saunders bounced off his porch as soon as he saw them and came running down the path.

"Hello!" he said cheerfully. "Where are you going? Do you like camping, Honey Bunch?"

"She hasn't camped yet," Frankie retorted

before Honey Bunch could say a word.
"Don't you have to go for the mail, Saunders?"

"Not yet—it's early," replied Saunders.
"If you are going to take a walk, I'll go with
you."

Of course, after that, there was nothing to
do but go on, and Saunders went, too.

Frankie whistled when they came to "Camp
Rest-Easy" where Jennie Kirk lived, but her
mother came out and told them she had gone
to the post-office and the store.

A few steps beyond Jennie's camp, they
came to another bungalow and a little girl and
boy, sitting on the lowest step, called out:

"Hello, Frankie Evans!"

"Well, here's the Foster twins," said
Frankie, who apparently knew every one at
Lake Tickaloc. "When did you come?"

"This morning," the little girl and boy answered.

Honey Bunch was sure they were twins—
they looked alike and spoke alike—and she
said she had twin cousins who lived in New
York. But these twins—their names were

Benny and Bertha—were only four years old.

"Stay and play," begged the twins.

Honey Bunch looked at Frankie—he was her guide.

"I don't mind—just a little while," said Frankie.

"We can have a tea party," the twins cried joyfully. "Mother's gone to see Aunt Nelly, but she lets us have crackers—animal crackers —and dates."

Honey Bunch didn't see how they could say everything together, but they did.

"You wait and we'll get the party," Benny and Bertha commanded. "Mother doesn't like lots of children in the house."

Honey Bunch and Frankie and Saunders sat down on the steps of the bungalow to wait, while the twins went around to the back door to go in the kitchen.

"The door's locked!" they cried, running back in a few minutes. "The wind locked it tight."

"Then we can't have any party," Saunders

grumbled. "I suppose everything you have to eat is inside the house."

"We can play something else," said Honey Bunch quickly. "We needn't play tea party."

The twins looked so troubled, Honey Bunch felt sorry for them.

"But we left the dog in the house," said Benny and Bertha. "Mother told us not to let him in, and we meant to put him out; but we didn't know the door was going to bang tight."

"Let me in a window and I'll open the door for you," Frankie offered.

He rather liked the idea of getting in at a window. He thought it would be exciting. He could play that he was a burglar and perhaps frighten the other children just a little, once he was in the house.

"All the windows are closed," Benny and Bertha announced, having run around the house to see.

"But they're not locked, are they?" asked Frankie. "Your mother wouldn't lock all the windows, would she?"

Honey Bunch saw that the twins were afraid it wasn't the right thing to do, to lock all the windows.

"My mother locks them at home," she declared. "When we go out to shop my mother locks all the windows downstairs. Even in the summer when it's hot."

"So does Mother," the twins said.

"Well, then, you'll have to wait till she comes home," Frankie retorted, as though that settled the matter.

Bertha Foster began to cry and Benny looked as though he might, too, in a minute.

"Oh, what's the matter?" asked Honey Bunch's little soft voice.

"The dog!" sobbed Bertha. "He will eat up the ginger cake that is getting cool on the kitchen table and Mother will scold."

"That's why she said not to let him in the house," Benny added.

Honey Bunch began to think quickly. Saunders and Frankie went to peer into the kitchen window, to see if they could see the ginger cake. They reported that it was still there.

"Isn't there anything but a window?" Honey Bunch asked suddenly.

Frankie giggled and wanted to know what she meant.

"I mean to get into the house with," explained Honey Bunch. "Like the chimney."

"Santa Claus comes down the chimney, but I don't think I could," Frankie said seriously. "Saunders couldn't, either."

"At home," declared Honey Bunch, "we have a little window, 'way down low, where we put in coal."

"Oh, we have one of those!" cried the Foster twins.

"Then couldn't you go through that?" Honey Bunch suggested to Frankie.

"Maybe," he answered. "Where is it?"

But the place for the coal chute was so small that Frankie could never hope to wriggle through it. He said so, as soon as he saw it.

"You go, Benny," he said to that twin.

"You can slip in there and cut upstairs and unlock the door in a jiffy."

"I don't want to—I'm afraid," Benny murmured, and Bertha began to cry and say he mustn't go.

"Then you go—you're little," Saunders told her.

But Bertha cried harder than ever at that suggestion.

"I'll go," said Honey Bunch. "I don't want the dog to eat the ginger cake. I can get through the hole, if you push me, Frankie."

Frankie at first did not want to push her, and he said she'd get her dress dirty. But at last he opened the little iron door and Honey Bunch began to wriggle through.

"I wonder—" she said, and then she disappeared from sight.

CHAPTER IX

NEW FRIENDS

THE reason Honey Bunch disappeared was because she had wriggled through the hole and tumbled down into the coal bin. She was surprised to find herself there, for she had not expected to tumble quite so quickly.

"I s'pose," she said to herself, "I'm rather dirty."

There was some coal in the bin, and though lumps of coal are not the pleasantest things to fall on, Honey Bunch was not hurt. It was lucky she couldn't see her face and hands and dress, however. The black coal had rubbed off on them until, as Mrs. Miller would have said, she was "a sight."

Honey Bunch stood up and wiped her hands on her dress.

"Where are the cellar stairs?" she called up to the hole where she could see one eye of

Bertha Foster and one eye of Frankie Evans.
They were both looking in at her.

"Over behind the furnace," called Bertha.
"You'll see them."

A strange cellar isn't so easy to get around
in as a cellar you know, like your own cellar,
we'll say. Honey Bunch fell over a soap box
and bumped her head on a rake that was hanging from a rafter before she found the stairs
that led up to the bungalow kitchen.

It was dark behind the heater, and Honey
Bunch had to feel her way. When she
reached the top of the stairs, she made an un-
pleasant discovery.

Slowly and carefully, she backed downstairs again and went over to the coal window.
There were no eyes peeping in at her.

"Frankie!" called Honey Bunch desper-
ately. "Bertha! Benny! Where are you?"

She heard a quick patter of feet and Frankie
Evans' face appeared at the little opening.

"We went around to the kitchen door to be
there when you opened it," he explained.
"What's the matter, Honey Bunch?"

"The cellar door is locked!" Honey Bunch said.

"Gee!" cried Frankie. "What a mess! Hey, Benny and Bertha," he called over his shoulder. "Come here, quick! Honey Bunch says the door to the cellar stairs is locked."

"Oh, my!" Honey Bunch heard Benny and Bertha say together.

"Can't she break the door down?" asked Saunders' voice.

Honey Bunch brushed a sooty hand across her forehead and left a long, black mark. She didn't feel like breaking down a door. She was sure Mrs. Foster would not like it.

"Of course she can't break down a door," Frankie protested. "She's too little."

"What shall I do?" asked Honey Bunch.

The twins and Frankie and Saunders didn't know what to say, so they said nothing.

"Go and see if the dog ate up the cake," Honey Bunch commanded.

Benny and Bertha ran to the kitchen window and peered in.

"The cake's all right," Honey Bunch heard
them cry.

They wanted her to come out of the cellar,
but she couldn't reach the coal window and
there was nothing to step on to help her.
Honey Bunch began to feel as if she might
cry. It was no fun to be locked in a strange
cellar.

"Maybe the door," she said to herself, "has
a catch."

She remembered how—oh, ever so long ago
—she and Tess Turner had hidden in a closet
when they were playing hide-and-go-seek.
The closet door had shut and the catch had
fastened it. Honey Bunch recollected that the
inside of the door had been smooth, but that
on the other side there was something to take
hold of.

"Has the cellar door a catch?" she called
through the window.

Benny and Bertha didn't know. Honey
Bunch giggled when she heard Frankie tell
them that they didn't know anything about
their own house.

"I'll go see," said Honey Bunch, who, warm and tired and breathless from so much shouting, as she was, was still not cross.

Up the stairs she trotted and felt around the door knob. There *was* something there—it made a little bump.

Honey Bunch pressed against it. Nothing happened. She pushed it sideways. Still the door refused to open. And then she jerked it down and the cellar door flew open so quickly that Honey Bunch fell over the top step and hurt her elbow.

"She's in!" shouted Frankie, who had been watching through the window.

Honey Bunch ran over and opened the kitchen door. The twins made Frankie and Saunders stay outside—they said their mother didn't like too many children in the house— and they rushed for the table.

There was the cake, just as Mrs. Foster had left it.

"Where's the dog?" asked Honey Bunch.

Having gone to all this trouble, she thought

she might at least be shown the dog who would
have eaten the cake if he had had a chance.

"He must be in the parlor," Benny and
Bertha declared, and they went in to look.

"Here he is!" they cried, and Honey Bunch
just had time to see a little white, curly-haired
dog being dragged off the sofa when a strange
voice came from the doorway.

"Whose little girl is this?" said the voice.

Honey Bunch turned around and saw a lady
standing in the hall. She knew she must be
the twins' mother.

"Why, I thought you were a little colored
girl!" Mrs. Foster exclaimed, and then she
began to laugh.

"What have you children been doing?" she
asked, as soon as she could stop laughing.

"We thought the dog would eat the cake, so
I climbed in through the coal window,"
Honey Bunch explained. "I s'pose I'm rather
dirty."

Mrs. Foster laughed again and led her into
a pretty green and white bathroom. There
was a mirror over the tub and she helped

Honey Bunch climb up on the rim and
steadied her while the little girl looked at herself.

Honey Bunch could scarcely believe her
eyes! Her face was almost as black as the
stove and streaked with perspiration. Her
eyes looked very queer, set in this odd black
face. Her dress was streaked and spotted, and
altogether she did not look like Honey Bunch
at all!

"I think it is a shame that you had to get
yourself in such a state, with two boys who
might have climbed in the window for you
standing right there," said Mrs. Foster, while
the twins peered in at the door and listened.

"They were too big," Honey Bunch explained, shutting her eyes, for Mrs. Foster had
dipped a cloth in warm water and was wash-
ing her face.

"Then they should not have let you do it,"
replied Mrs. Foster, letting water run into the
basin for Honey Bunch's hands.

By the time her face and hands were washed
and her hair brushed, Honey Bunch looked

more like herself. Some of the coal dust shook
off her dress and, as Mrs. Foster said, it would
wash and no one need worry about a wash
dress.

Then she insisted on cutting the ginger cake
and each youngster had a piece, even
"Toodles," the poodle, who was very fond of
cake. He was so fond of it that he sometimes
climbed up on the table and ate it without asking.

When the cake was finished, Saunders said
he had to go to the post-office, but Frankie
wanted to show Honey Bunch more of the
camps. The twins wanted to go, too, so they
set out for Dora Green's camp, which was
known as Camp Birches.

A little girl came flying out of the tent between the birch trees when they came to this
camp. She ran to Honey Bunch.

"You dear, darling Honey Bunch!" she exclaimed. "I'm so glad to see you! My mother
is coming over to see your mother to-morrow
afternoon."

The next minute Jessie Waller came run-

ning up with Jennie Kirk, and they were so
glad to see Honey Bunch that they told her so
"over and over," as Frankie said.

"Why do you keep saying the same thing?"
he asked impatiently.

Mrs. Green laughed and said that that was
the way girls always talked.

"Where's your doll?" asked Jennie Kirk
eagerly. "Did you bring her with you?"

And the twins edged up close to Honey
Bunch and stared hopefully. They wanted
to see the doll, too.

"I left Ida Grace at the camp," Honey
Bunch said. "But I'll show her to you, if
you'll come back and want to play with her."

"We'll come to-morrow," promised Jennie
and Jessie and Dora. "We have to go in swimming now."

The twins said they would come to-morrow
too, to see the doll, and they walked back as
far as their own camp with Honey Bunch and
Frankie.

"So long! See you to-morrow," said
Frankie, leaving Honey Bunch at her tent

door. "You'll like camping out, Honey
Bunch; it's lots of fun."

Honey Bunch was sure it was when she ate
her supper outdoors that night and drank her
milk from a tin cup. Her mother and
daddy had coffee, and the coffee pot sat over
a fire of sticks, for they were using the stone
fireplace. But the very nicest part of that
very nice day—nice in spite of her adventure
in the coal cellar—happened at the end of it.

After supper, Mr. Morton said they must
light their first campfire, and he gave Honey
Bunch a little flaming torch and held back her
skirts while she carefully set fire to the dry
twigs he had heaped in a mound. When the
fire was burning briskly, he put on several
logs. All around the lake campfires were
blazing. Honey Bunch, with Mother's help,
could count ten. It was cool enough to wear
a sweater, for a keen wind had blown over the
lake as soon as the sun had gone down, and
the heat from the fire felt most comfortable.

"Isn't it nice to camp out?" said Honey
Bunch, sitting in her mother's lap and watch-

ing the fire wink and crackle before her eyes. "Norman would like to camp out here. I know he would."

Thinking of Norman made Honey Bunch remember the wildcats, and she glanced a little fearfully over her mother's shoulder. The fire threw queer, long shadows and they moved so much that Honey Bunch almost thought one of them might be a wildcat's shadow!

"Do you suppose there *are* any wildcats up here, Daddy?" she asked, trying to pretend that she didn't care whether there were or not.

"Nonsense!" answered her daddy. "I don't believe in wildcats, myself. But, Honey Bunch, I have always heard that this is a great place for fairies!"

Honey Bunch sat up, her eyes big and round.

"Oh, my!" she whispered. "Fairies! Are —are there any here now, Daddy?"

"I don't know," her daddy answered, putting another log on the fire; "but I shouldn't be surprised if there were. They may be hidden in the grass, listening to us."

Honey Bunch snuggled down into her mother's lap, her eyes shining.

"Tell me about them, Daddy," she begged. "Tell about the fairies."

"The Lake Tickaloc fairies," began Daddy Morton seriously, "are divided into two bands —there are the water fairies and the land fairies. The land fairies always wear green dresses, while the water fairies are dressed in shimmering white. They are cousins—yes, that's right, cousins. And every summer the land fairies appoint one of their number to be the good fairy for each camp. For instance, I think Frankie Evans has a good fairy in his camp."

"Have we a good fairy in our camp, Daddy?" asked Honey Bunch, sitting up so suddenly she bumped her head against her mother's chin.

"To be sure," replied Daddy Morton.

"Oh, Daddy, are you teasing?" Honey Bunch cried. "I do think you're teasing me,

Daddy Morton! What is the fairy's name?"

"Moonbeam Violet Leaf," said Daddy Morton so promptly that Honey Bunch blinked.

Think of knowing a fairy's name!

"Have you ever seen her?" Honey Bunch asked eagerly. "Have you ever seen Moonbeam Violet Leaf, Daddy?"

Honey Bunch waited anxiously for her daddy's reply. She had never seen a fairy, but she had always wanted to know how one looked.

"Oh, no, I never *saw* Moonbeam Violet Leaf," answered Daddy Morton, and he seemed to be shocked at the idea. "You know, Honey Bunch, that fairies do not like to be seen; they hide away during the day and come out at night after mortals are in bed. I dare say Fairy Leaf will come out to-night after we leave the campfire."

"Why do you call her Fairy Leaf?" asked Honey Bunch curiously.

"Because she has such a long name," Daddy Morton explained. "Just as I call you 'Honey

Bunch' instead of Gertrude Marion Morton."

Honey Bunch nodded. She was staring at something.

"Look, Daddy!" she whispered mysteriously. "Look, Mother! Over there by that tree! See that leaf all curled over? It moved. Maybe Fairy Leaf is hiding under there."

"I shouldn't be surprised," Mrs. Morton whispered back. "Perhaps she thinks it is time we went to bed. Let's go as quietly as we can and we won't disturb her. Daddy will cover up the fire."

So Honey Bunch stood up and took her mother's hand and together they tiptoed into the tent. They went so quietly that I do not believe even a fairy could have heard them. Honey Bunch took a hurried little peep at the leaf as she passed it, and what do you think? Something fluffy and soft stuck out of it. Honey Bunch was sure it must be the dress of the fairy, Moonbeam Violet Leaf.

CHAPTER X

A FAIRY'S PRESENT

ALL the time she was undressing, Honey
Bunch thought about the fairies. It was lovely
to think that they were outside the tent and
would be playing around Camp Snapdragon
all night. Nothing could happen in a camp
where the fairies were! Norman's wildcats
that he talked so much about would never dare
come near them!

When Honey Bunch woke in the morning
there was a surprise for her. She shrieked
with delight and her daddy and mother came
hurrying to see what was the matter.

"Look!" cried Honey Bunch, hopping up
and down as she always did when anything
surprised and pleased her. "Look! Moonbeam Violet Leaf forgot her cup and saucer!"

Sure enough, it did look that way. There,
right on the very edge of the tent floor—where

you couldn't miss seeing it and where any one would have stepped on it who wasn't a fairy —was an acorn cup and saucer. Just one acorn cup and saucer, as if a fairy had been drinking tea and left in a hurry.

"Is it the fairy's cup and saucer, Mother?" begged Honey Bunch. "Is it, really? Where did it come from?"

Mrs. Morton took the tiny cup and saucer and turned it over. My goodness, there on the bottom of the saucer were the tiniest initials you ever saw!

"M. V. L." they said.

"I want to show Jessie and Dora and Jennie," said the excited Honey Bunch. "I never saw a real cup and saucer that a fairy had used before. Do you suppose Fairy Leaf will come back to-night to get it, Mother?"

Mrs. Morton said she didn't know, but that if Honey Bunch would take good care of the cup and saucer and not break it, it would be easy to give it back again.

"We'll leave it in the same place when we go to bed, and if the fairy wants it, she will take it," Mrs. Morton declared. "If she leaves it, I think that will mean she is willing for you to have it, Honey Bunch."

It did seem to Honey Bunch that no matter what she wanted to do, there was always breakfast to be eaten. However, she put the acorn cup and saucer close to her cereal bowl and she looked at it while she ate, so that made it easier. And before she had finished drying the dishes for Mother—Honey Bunch could dry dishes nicely and she liked to help her mother with everything she did (have you ever heard of the famous pie Honey Bunch baked one baking day and what happened to it?)—Jennie Kirk and Dora Green and Jennie Waller were seen coming up the road.

"Could we see your doll now and play with her a little?" asked Dora.

Honey Bunch took Ida Grace under her arm and gave the suitcase to Jennie to carry. She took the acorn cup and saucer herself.

"Mother said it was nice out under the trees," she said. "Let's go there to play."

And as soon as they were seated on the grass,

Honey Bunch showed the girls the fairy cup
and saucer.

"My goodness!" said Jennie, her eyes dancing. "Isn't that too lovely for anything! A
fairy never left anything for me. What are
you going to do with it, Honey Bunch?"

"I'll put it where Moonbeam Violet Leaf
can have it back, if she wants it," Honey
Bunch replied. "But if she doesn't take it, I
am going to keep it."

"Well, I'll be over the first thing in the
morning," promised Dora. "I want to see if
she takes it back."

The girls examined the cup and saucer very
carefully and saw the initials, and then Honey
Bunch carried it back to the tent and her
mother put it away for her. After that they
played with Ida Grace and tried all her
clothes on her, and Dora and Jessie and Jennie
told Honey Bunch about their dolls at home.

"Put Ida Grace away, quick!" said Jessie
suddenly. "Here comes Frankie Evans with
the Lambert dog."

Honey Bunch looked up and saw Frankie.

At his heels was a shaggy dog with friendly brown eyes and a rather tangled coat of hair. He looked as though he had not been brushed or combed very lately.

"Hello!" said Frankie.

"Is that your dog?" Honey Bunch asked eagerly. She liked dogs.

"No, that isn't anybody's dog," Jessie answered, before Frankie could say a word. "He lives with the Lamberts—they keep the store next to the post-office—but he doesn't belong to them. Some people were up here one summer and they went away and left Rover."

"I think that was mean!" declared Honey Bunch. "I wouldn't go away and leave Lady Clare. Not unless I told her about it and told her when I was coming back."

"My mother said it was mean, too," Jennie Kirk announced. "But Rover has a good time. He goes all around the lake and people feed him."

Honey Bunch patted the dog and he wagged his tail. Then he lay down in the grass, his red tongue hanging out. He had walked far that morning, and he was warm.

"He takes things!" said Jessie. "He ran off with Mrs. Taylor's knitting bag once and she never found it. And he stole the robe out of an automobile once."

"Well, Mrs. Napoleon found that," Frankie retorted. "Rover doesn't mean to steal things; he does it for fun."

"I told Honey Bunch to put her doll away," said Jessie. "Rover might run off with that."

"No, he wouldn't," Frankie argued. "Look at him looking at you! He knows you are saying things about him!"

Sure enough, Rover had his brown eyes fixed on Jessie's face. He seemed almost ready to cry.

"I didn't mean anything, Rover," apologized Jessie hastily, patting him on his shaggy head. "I hope I didn't hurt your feelings."

Rover looked more cheerful.

"That's all right," he seemed to say, as he wagged his tail, thumping it on the grass. "That's all right. No harm done."

"Are you going in swimming?" asked
Frankie. "We are, at eleven o'clock."

"So are we," said Dora. "Everybody is."

And nearly everybody was, Honey Bunch
discovered, when she asked her daddy. Mrs.
Morton did not want to go, but Honey Bunch
and her daddy put on their bathing suits and
they took the china doll with them.

"Hello, Honey Bunch!" called Jennie Kirk,
dancing up in a bright red suit. "Did you
bring the china doll?"

Honey Bunch had brought the china doll,
in her own bathing suit, and when the other
children saw her and the string tied to her so
that she could really swim in the water, they
crowded around and wanted to take her swimming.

"Let me!" Saunders Abbott cried loudly.
"Let me take your doll swimming, Honey
Bunch."

"Don't let him!" whispered Dora Green,
whose bathing suit matched her name—it was
green and white. "He will break it or lose it
or something."

Honey Bunch had the same feeling, but she did not say so. She just looked at Saunders gravely, with her blue eyes, and said gently:

"I shouldn't think you would like to play with dolls, Saunders."

A big boy, sitting on the wharf, laughed, and Saunders flushed angrily.

"I wouldn't touch your old doll!" he said crossly, and dived into the water.

Honey Bunch didn't want him to be cross, but she was glad he did not have her doll. She had asked her daddy not to take her into the lake "the first minute," and he had promised that she should not go in till she was ready. So Honey Bunch and Dora and Jennie and Jessie "sailed" the china doll up and down, pulling her by the string as they stood on the wharf. When Jennie leaned too far over and lost her balance, no one cried out when she fell in. The water was not deep and she came up laughing.

"It's warm to-day," she said. "I like it when it's warm."

"If I'm not mistaken, we are going to have

a storm soon," Honey Bunch heard one of the men saying. "Probably reach us by to-morrow. We have had clear weather for three weeks now and a change is about due."

"Ready to go in, Daughter?" asked Honey Bunch's daddy presently.

He was swimming around at the end of the wharf and he seemed to be having such a good time that Honey Bunch made up her mind she would like to do that, too. So he held out his arms and she jumped down into them. For just one moment she thought Jennie had been mistaken about the water—it felt so cold! Then she was used to it and splashing her daddy as joyously as he splashed her.

"It doesn't taste like the ocean," said Honey Bunch, when she swallowed a mouthful. "Does it, Daddy?"

"It isn't like the ocean," Daddy Morton explained. "That is salt water and this is fresh; some people call it 'sweet' water. There is no salt in it."

Honey Bunch swam a little—she had begun to learn when she visited her cousin Julie at

the seashore. She paddled with Jessie and
Dora and Jennie. She climbed up on the
wharf and jumped off. In fact she did all the
things the other children did and had a beautiful time.

"I *like* it!" she kept saying, as she and her
daddy went back to their camp to dress and
get their dinner. "I *like* it here!"

Well, so she did, and it was no wonder.
Mrs. Morton had a delicious dinner all ready
for them, and after that, while Mother took a
nap, Honey Bunch went rowing with her
daddy on the lake. They took Ida Grace.
Mrs. Napoleon in her launch passed them and
stopped to speak. The baby, Charles Augustus, and Mrs. Hendricks were in the launch,
too, and Mrs. Hendricks promised to knit a
sweater for Ida Grace.

"These cool evenings she will need one, and
I have some blue wool I didn't know how to
use up," she said. "There is just about enough
for a doll's sweater, I am sure."

After the row on the lake, Honey Bunch
went with her mother to get the mail, and

there was a letter from Mrs. Miller saying
that Lady Clare was well and sent her love.
Honey Bunch and her mother stopped at a
house and bought some fresh eggs for breakfast, and the woman said that she thought a
storm was coming.

"My bones tell me," she declared, and
Honey Bunch wished she had that kind of
bones.

"My bones don't tell me a thing!" she said
on the way home.

They built another campfire that night and
Honey Bunch heard more about the fairies
and especially about Moonbeam Violet Leaf.

"I must leave the cup and saucer right in
the doorway for her," said Honey Bunch,
when it was time to go to bed.

CHAPTER XI

WHEN THE WIND BLEW

BEFORE Honey Bunch was tucked into her cot she put the acorn cup and saucer on the floor, in the doorway of the tent. She hoped the fairy would not take it away; but perhaps she would need it for her set of dishes. Honey Bunch remembered how bad mother had felt when Mrs. Miller broke a cup and saucer that belonged to her best set of dishes and it must be almost as bad to lose a cup and saucer as to have it broken.

"Perhaps I'll wake up and *see* her take it," murmured Honey Bunch, as she drifted off into the land of dreams.

But playing outdoors all day long makes little girls mighty sleepy, and Honey Bunch did not wake till the sunshine was coming through the doorway of the tent and the fire was built and breakfast almost ready.

"Did Moonbeam Violet Leaf come and take her cup and saucer?" cried Honey Bunch, jumping from the cot and running to look.

Mr. Morton had stepped carefully around the cup and saucer, for it was still there. And there was something else there. A tiny, tiny red napkin, about as large as a piece of taffy— you know how large a square of taffy is— fringed all around.

"Mother!" squealed Honey Bunch, in delight. "Mothe-r! The fairy has left a napkin. And I don't believe she wants the cup and saucer."

Mr. and Mrs. Morton said that they thought the fairy must want Honey Bunch to have these things, and so it seemed. For, would you believe it? every single night of their stay in camp, the fairies left something for Honey Bunch. Sometimes it was a cup and saucer, like the first one; once it was an acorn teapot; one night it was a set of dishes all made from leaves. Not a night passed that something wasn't left, and every morning the other children in camp came over to see what the gift

was. It was strange, but the fairies did not
leave things at the other camps. Jennie Kirk
said that Honey Bunch was "lucky."

This morning, Honey Bunch knew exactly
what she was going to do. She and Jennie had
planned to pick pine needles to fill the pillow-
cover Ida Camp had given to Honey Bunch.
Jennie had heard all about Ida Camp. Indeed she knew by name the girls in Barham
who lived on Grove Street near the Mortons,
for Honey Bunch had told her all about her
friends.

"I'd like to take Ida Grace," said Honey
Bunch, bringing out the doll when Jennie
came for her. "See, she has on her khaki suit."

Sure enough, the doll wore the khaki blouse
and bloomers and she looked very much like
Honey Bunch except, of course, she was much
smaller.

"Doesn't she look cunning?" said Jennie.
"She is the nicest doll I ever saw."

Dora and Jessie said the same thing when
they came hurrying up a few minutes later.
As they always wanted to go everywhere

Honey Bunch went, no one was much surprised to see Benny and Bertha Foster running down the road a few minutes after they had started for the pine woods back of the camps.

"Let us go with you?" called Benny and Bertha, as usual speaking together. "Mother said we could go."

Honey Bunch smiled and waved her hand. Dora, who was looking ahead, giggled.

"Here comes Frankie Evans," she reported. "Rover is with him."

Frankie was whistling, and there were three other boys with him. Mrs. Morton, hanging out dish towels, saw them and laughed.

"If they all pick pine needles, Honey Bunch will have enough for a dozen pillows," she said to Mr. Morton.

"Hello," Frankie greeted the little girls and Benny. "These are the Hammer boys. They came yesterday. He's Dick and this is Fred and that is Albert."

The Hammer boys ducked their heads and grinned. They were about Frankie's age, and Honey Bunch liked them because they were good to Rover. They patted him every other minute and spoke to him as though they loved him already.

"We're going to the woods to get pine needles to go in this pillow," explained Honey Bunch.

"My daddy says it is going to storm," Frankie announced. "But lots of time the storms blow over, up here. Do you mind if we come, Honey Bunch?"

"No, I think it will be nice," Honey Bunch answered. "You can pick pine needles and make your mother a pillow."

So there were ten children who tramped along merrily, and they were so interested in what they were saying that when the sun went behind a cloud they never noticed that it had disappeared.

"I wonder if there are any wild animals up here," Albert Hammer said, looking through the trees as though he rather expected to meet a bear.

"No! Of course not!" replied Frankie scornfully. "How silly you are! There wouldn't be any wild animals where there are so many people."

"Norman Clark—he is a boy who lives next door to me at home—said there would be wild-cats," Honey Bunch declared.

"Gee, I wouldn't mind seeing a wildcat," Dick Hammer said eagerly. "That would be fun. I have an air gun and I might be able to hit him."

"Well, you won't see any, because there aren't any to see," the sensible Dora Green informed him. "We have been up here for lots of summers, and we never saw any."

When the children came to the grove where the ground was slippery with dried pine needles, Bertha Foster wanted to hold Ida Grace. Honey Bunch put the doll in the little girl's arms and the other children began to gather up the fragrant pine.

"Say, that's a cold wind. Did you feel it?" Frankie asked suddenly.

"Come see what I've found!" shouted Fred Hammer, and no one thought about the wind, but rushed to the spot where Fred was standing.

Bertha propped Ida Grace up against the tree and came running, too. Fred had found a turtle, and Honey Bunch told them about the turtle she had found and taken to her cousin Julie at the seashore. They were still looking at the turtle, and Fred had decided to take it back to their camp for a mascot, when a spatter of rain fell on Honey Bunch's hand.

"It's raining!" she cried, in surprise.

Then, without warning, the wind began to blow and the trees made such a moaning sound that the twins were frightened and began to cry.

"We'd better hurry," said Frankie. "I'm glad we didn't go into the grove very far. Take hold of hands and run."

The children took hold of hands and raced for the camps. The wind and rain struck them with full force as they came out of the grove, but rain never hurts a child and they were all used to getting wet in the summer time.

Honey Bunch shut her eyes and let Frankie

and Dick pull her along. They stopped so
suddenly that she nearly lost her balance.

"This isn't the right road!" Frankie declared.

"I tried to tell you that!" gasped Jennie.
"But you wouldn't listen."

"Didn't hear you," said Frankie briefly.

"This is the long way around," Jessie announced. "I know the road. We'll be
drowned, if we go this way."

"Get your breaths," ordered Frankie, "and
then we'll go back."

He waited a few minutes and then, taking
hands again, they started back. The wind was
at their backs and helped them along and they
were so thoroughly wet that splashing into
puddles couldn't possibly hurt them. Frankie
knew the right way now, and they came to the
camps just as Mrs. Morton was starting her
husband off to look for Honey Bunch.

The other children dashed on to their own
tents and Honey Bunch was put into dry
clothes and the rest of the day, after lunch,
she spent watching the storm and writing a

letter to Ida Camp—that is, Mother wrote it
and Honey Bunch told her what to say. Then
Mrs. Morton read aloud to her little daughter
till it was supper time.

It was the most terrific storm that had swept
Lake Tickaloc that summer, and some people
said they had never seen a storm like it. The
wind lashed the trees and the flags that were
left flying and drove the rain across the
wharves in sheets.

"We had a cold lunch and we'll have to
have a cold supper," said Mrs. Morton. "We
can't have a fire in a storm like this."

Luckily there was plenty of food cooked
and in cans, and Honey Bunch thought it was
fun—a new kind of picnic—to eat her supper
just as her mother handed it to her, one thing
at a time.

After supper, Daddy Morton lit two lamps
that swung from the center pole of the tent.
He and Honey Bunch liked to play tit-tat-toe,
but Mrs. Morton said she had to sew a button
on a dress for Honey Bunch. The tent shook
and rattled in the wind, but Larry had water-

proofed the canvas thoroughly and no rain
came through.

"The lamp's going out," said Honey Bunch
suddenly.

One of the lamps flickered and died out that
very minute.

"I'll watch you play," Mrs. Morton decided, putting down her sewing. "No one
wants to go outdoors and get any more kero-
sene."

"Will—will the tent blow down?" asked
Honey Bunch, forgetting her game.

"I hardly think so," Daddy Morton said
cheerfully. "If it does, we'll go to Mrs.
Applegate's. Bungalows do not blow away."

Honey Bunch won a game of tit-tat-toe and
she was so excited she almost forgot the storm.
But when she heard something snap, she remembered.

"What was that?" she cried. "I heard it."

Mr. and Mrs. Morton had heard the snap-
ping noise, too.

Snap! it sounded again.

"It was almost like a pistol shot," said Mrs.

Morton, rising. "But no one would be firing a pistol around here."

"The tent's blowing down!" Honey Bunch cried, pointing to one corner. "Look, Daddy, the tent's blowing down!"

Her father shook his head.

"I know what has happened," he said quietly. "Those two tent pegs I made of green wood have snapped. That means two of the strings have given way. I'll have to go out and see what I can do."

The tent was sagging, just a little, over in the corner to which Honey Bunch had pointed. The wind was making the canvas ripple in and out, and no wonder the little girl thought the tent was blowing down.

"I'll have to take the lamp," said Mr. Morton. "The lantern is out where the stove is. You won't be afraid to stay in the dark a few minutes, will you?"

Honey Bunch and her mother said "no indeed" and Mr. Morton took down the other lamp—the one that was still lit—and went outdoors. He was back before they expected him.

"I'll have to have two pegs, Edith," he said to Mrs. Morton. "Is there anything I can use?"

Mrs. Morton brought him the broom and he took out a little saw from the small tool chest he kept under his cot and sawed the broomstick in two pieces. Then he took the lamp and went out again.

"Edith!" he called in a moment, "can you come out and help me? It isn't raining so hard now."

Mrs. Morton, holding Honey Bunch tightly by the hand, felt her way to the tent flap.

"Wait here for Mother, dear," she said, and went around to the other side where Honey Bunch's daddy was working.

Honey Bunch looked over her shoulder at the dark tent and then out into the still darker night. She felt like a very little girl indeed.

"Perhaps my daddy needs me, too," she said to herself.

She thought she heard a noise in the tent and she started to run. Her foot caught in something and down she went.

"Mother!" screamed Honey Bunch. "Mother!"

Mrs. Morton reached her in less than a second and picked her up.

"Did you fall over a tent rope, darling?" she asked. "Never mind—you are not hurt and Daddy has the pegs fixed."

Honey Bunch was glad to see the lamp again and glad, too, to go to bed. Her daddy said the tent couldn't blow down now and that, anyway, the wind and rain were dying down. Honey Bunch felt very cozy and secure in her cot—as long as Mother and Daddy were with her—and she stayed awake a little while, listening to the sound of the rain and wondering if she could go out to play the next day.

Some time during the night the rain stopped, and that was probably why Moonbeam Violet Leaf could get to the tent to leave her present. This time Honey Bunch found a long necklace of plaited grass stems, just the kind of ornament a fairy would wear. Honey Bunch wished she knew how to make one.

"It would be nice for Ida Grace to wear

when she is dressed up," said Honey Bunch, hopping outdoors to see the sunshine.

It was a beautiful morning and the sun was smiling as though there had never been a storm. But Honey Bunch came up to her mother, who was making coffee for breakfast, with such a sober face that Mrs. Morton was afraid she did not feel well.

"What is the matter, darling?" she asked. "Did the rain keep you awake?"

"No-o," said Honey Bunch. "It's Ida Grace."

"Ida Grace?" repeated Mrs. Morton. "Why, what is the matter with Ida Grace? I thought she was having a good time in camp."

"She's lost!" Honey Bunch sobbed. "I must have left her in the woods. I took her yesterday morning and I forgot to bring her home."

Well, nothing is ever as bad, or as sad, as you think it is, after you have told your mother about it. You've noticed that? As soon as Mrs. Morton heard about Ida Grace, she thought of something that Honey Bunch had not.

"If Bertha Foster was playing with her, she probably took her home, dear," said Mrs. Morton. "The storm excited you and you would not see whether Bertha carried the doll or not. As soon as you've had breakfast, you run over there and ask Bertha if she hasn't Ida Grace."

After breakfast Honey Bunch went over to the camp where the Foster twins lived, but their aunt said they were down on the wharf watching the wrecked boats being towed ashore.

"A doll?" repeated their Aunt Lottie, when Honey Bunch asked her if Bertha had brought home a doll with her the day before. "No, dear, I didn't see any doll. Bertha would have told us, I am sure, if she had a doll that wasn't hers."

Honey Bunch hurried down toward the wharf. Before she reached it, she met Jennie Kirk. Jennie was sorry to hear that Ida Grace was lost, but when Honey Bunch told her what her mother had said about Bertha taking the doll home, Jennie felt better. She said she was sure that was what had happened and that the aunt might not have seen Ida Grace.

"Did you take Ida Grace home with you?" Honey Bunch asked anxiously, as soon as they found the Foster twins on the wharf.

Bertha and Benny stared. They were only four years old, and sometimes one had to ask them a question more than once before they understood. But they understood this question the very first time.

"Rover ran off with your doll!" they said, speaking together. "Didn't you see him, Honey Bunch? He ran ahead of us, through the woods."

"He had Ida Grace in his mouth," added Bertha.

CHAPTER XII

CARNIVAL DAY

Poor Honey Bunch stared at the twins and they stared back. But Jennie Kirk stamped her foot.

"Why didn't you say *something?*" she demanded. "Didn't you know any better than to let that dog run off with Honey Bunch's best doll?"

"We did say something," the twins protested. "We said 'look—look'; but Frankie jerked us and said to keep still and run.

There was no use scolding the twins, for this was exactly what had happened. Frankie, eager to get the younger children home safely, had hurried them along, and, if they tried to say something, had urged them to keep still and use their breath for running.

Perhaps we can find Ida Grace," said Jennie

hopefully. "We'll go look in the pine grove. Rover may have dropped her."

Honey Bunch had not much hope of this, but she followed Jennie. The Foster twins went, too. They searched through the pine grove and found the place where they had stopped to look at the turtle, but there was no sign of Ida Grace. When Frankie heard she was lost, he searched, too, and so did Mr. Morton. They tried to get Rover to take them to the places where he buried his bones—for they thought he might have hidden Ida Grace—but Rover merely wagged his tail and looked foolish.

"I am afraid Ida Grace is lost, dear, but you mustn't feel too bad," said Mrs. Morton, when the doll had been missing two days and nearly every one on the lake had tried to find her. "Try to think of something else. Eleanor will be waiting for you when you go home and we'll pretend that Rover took Ida Grace to some poor little girl who didn't have any doll."

Honey Bunch began to think of this little

girl, and she gave her a name—Rose—and
after a while she began to believe that Ida
Grace was Rose's doll. Frankie went hunting
every now and then for the lost doll. He felt
he was to blame that Rover had carried her
off, for Rover was really Frankie's dog during
the summer—but he never found her.

Then every one began to talk of the boat
races on Carnival Day, and, in the excitement,
Ida Grace was almost forgotten.

"They have a boat parade on the lake on
Labor Day," Honey Bunch asked her mother
to write to Mrs. Miller. "Daddy is going to
take me to our wharf and we can see them all
go by. And they have races, too. There is a
boy's race and Frankie Evans is going to row
a boat in that."

All the children were interested in the rowboat races. Frankie was so small and slight
that when he was in a rowboat only the top of
his dark head showed. Of course he could not
row one of the heavy boats, but his father had
had a light boat built especially for him and
the Hammer boys had another. Honey

Bunch made every one in the post-office laugh one afternoon when she spoke of the boat races.

"I hope Frankie beats the Tack boys," she told the postmaster.

"The Tack boys?" the postmaster repeated. "I didn't know we had a family by that name up here. Where's their camp, Honey Bunch?"

"It's between the Evans' and the Kirks'," explained Honey Bunch eagerly.

"Are you sure you don't mean the Hammer boys, then?" the postmaster asked, his eyes twinkling.

Honey Bunch laughed as heartily as the people who were listening, and the three Hammer boys laughed, too, when she told them.

"Once we had a teacher in school who called us everything in the tool chest, except the right name," said Albert. "One week we would be the Saw boys and the next week she'd call us the three Chisels. You couldn't blame her so much, because there was another boy in the class whose name was Hatchett. I guess names are hard to remember, anyway."

Honey Bunch by this time knew practically every one in camp and every one who lived near there. She and Frankie often went to see the baby, Charles Augustus. Mrs. Hendricks finished the sweater for Ida Grace, and she had insisted that Honey Bunch should put it away.

"You may find Ida Grace," Mrs. Hendricks insisted. "If you don't, let one of your other dolls wear the sweater."

Honey Bunch knew how all the boats were to be trimmed for Labor Day and what the prizes were to be. The judges invited her to stand on their float with them and see the water carnival.

"But I would rather have my little girl safe on dry land, with Daddy," said Mrs. Morton. "You can see everything from the wharf and you will not be crowded."

Honey Bunch was quite willing to stay on the wharf. She knew that Saunders Abbott would be on the float—his cousin was one of

the judges—and it was never altogether comfortable for Honey Bunch where that boy was.
He always teased her, and though she did not
dislike him and sometimes felt sorry for him,
Honey Bunch knew that she would have a better time alone with her daddy.

Carnival Day was the most exciting day in
the year at Lake Tickaloc. The campers began the day with a picnic that started in the
morning and lasted till three o'clock, when the
boat parade began. There was a huge fire
built, and every one brought plenty to eat and
laughed and visited until parade time. Then
a great many of the people went out into the
middle of the lake and anchored their boats
and watched the parade from there.

Others stayed on their own wharfs, and fully
half the campers entered a boat in the carnival
or in the races. Mr. and Mrs. Morton declared that they would rather look on, and
they went down to the wharf soon after three
with Honey Bunch to watch the boats.

"That's Mrs. Napoleon's boat," said Honey

Bunch, as the long line of flag-decked boats
started to come down the lake.

Honey Bunch knew every boat, for she had
seen them being trimmed. Mrs. Napoleon's
launch looked like Fairyland, for it was all
silver and white, and Charles Augustus, half
smothered in white asters, rode in the prow.
His mother was holding him so he would not
fall off, but you could not see her. From
where Honey Bunch stood it looked as though
the baby was alone on the boat.

"Are there water fairies on Mrs. Napoleon's boat, Daddy?" Honey Bunch asked,
remembering what her daddy had told her of
the land fairies and the water fairies.

"I shouldn't be surprised," replied Mr.
Morton. "Perhaps they are making Charles
Augustus laugh."

The baby was cooing and clapping his
hands, and Honey Bunch was sure the water
fairies must be singing to him.

"That is the Kirks' boat," said Honey
Bunch, when a boat that looked like a pumpkin came along.

Jennie was dressed as the Princess Cinderella and she rode in her pumpkin coach which had been built over a rowboat. Her daddy was rowing her, but the shell of the pumpkin hid him. It was a very pretty float, and afterward Honey Bunch was delighted to hear that Jennie had taken the second prize.

"Oh—oh—ah!" cried every one when another boat came in sight.

Honey Bunch stared, her blue eyes shining. She had never seen anything so pretty in her life.

"Mother!" she cried. "Oh, Mother! That is the secret boat!"

There had been just one boat which Honey Bunch had not seen. She knew more about it than any one else, though, for she knew it *was* a secret, and no one else guessed that such an exciting thing as a secret was being planned in the old boathouse at the head of the lake. Larry Bert had been working every night on the float for a week, and he had entered it for his mother.

"It's a duck!" said Honey Bunch, when she

had stared a few minutes at the boat, which
rather puzzled her.

Mr. Morton laughed and said it wasn't a
duck, but that Honey Bunch had guessed almost right.

"It is a swan, dear," he explained. "You
saw swans in the park in New York, you remember. You told me about those big white
birds with the long necks and how easily they
sailed on the water."

"Oh, yes, it is a swan, isn't it?" and Honey
Bunch nodded. "I hope Larry's mother gets
the prize."

The boat, from a little distance, looked like
a huge, graceful swan. Larry had managed to
hide every bit of the boat with the white
plumage, and he rowed so slowly that it moved
through the water no faster than a swan would
drift. From where Honey Bunch stood, she
could hear a soft clapping of hands from the
people who were in the boats, watching, and
those standing on the wharves.

"Wouldn't it be too nice if Larry did get
first prize?" said Honey Bunch. "I saw the

prizes in the grocery store window. The first prize for a float is a lamp. Mrs. Bert could use a lamp in their house."

That night, when the judges announced their decisions, Honey Bunch was to find that Larry's boat *had* won the first prize and that he carried home the lamp to his mother, who was so proud of it she wouldn't use it except on Larry's birthday and at Christmas time.

But of course Honey Bunch didn't hear this good news until hours later. In the meantime, the parade came to an end and the lake was cleared for the boat races.

These were very exciting, and Mr. Morton had to hold Honey Bunch by the belt of her sweater to keep her from falling off the wharf. She was so interested she kept stepping nearer to the edge at every race. The sweater was the same color as the one Mrs. Hendricks had knit for Ida Grace. Every time Honey Bunch looked at the sweater Mrs. Hendricks had made for Ida Grace, she wanted to cry. There it was, in the trunk, a lovely little blue sweater, and there was no dolly to wear it.

But Honey Bunch was not thinking of Ida Grace while she watched the boat races. She was wishing that they would hurry and get through so that Frankie Evans could row. Before the rowboat races for the boys, though, came the canoe and sailboat races and a motor boat sprint.

"There's a man selling something," said Mrs. Morton during the canoe race.

"Little boats!" cried Honey Bunch whose quick eyes had spied what the man had in his basket. Oh-oh, Mother! See—little boats!"

The man came down to the wharf, smiling.

"Boats?" he said, showing beautifully even white teeth as he smiled. "Boats for the little lady?"

"Why, Honey Bunch," Mr. Morton declared teasingly, "little girls don't play with boats, do they?"

"Yes they do, Daddy," said Honey Bunch anxiously. "Look, he has a rowboat like Frankie's, and a canoe and a sailboat—and everything!"

And Honey Bunch stood on tiptoe to see

into the basket and gently touched each boat with her little pointed finger.

"Which one do you want, dear?" her daddy asked. He liked to tease his little girl sometimes, but he always knew when she really wanted something very much.

"Could I have the canoe?" said Honey Bunch.

"All right, you take that, and we'll get Frankie a rowboat and perhaps a sailboat to take home to Norman," Mr. Morton decided.

Then he paid for the boats and put them in his pocket, for they were tiny boats, and the dark-skinned man with his basket went off to sell more boats.

"Now we'll have to pay attention to the races, or we'll miss Frankie," said Mrs. Morton.

Before the boys' races began they had a tug of war. Honey Bunch thought this was very interesting. Half a dozen men got into one rowboat and half a dozen climbed into another and they took a long rope and pulled, to see which boat could take it away from the other.

"Why do they wear their bathing suits?" asked Honey Bunch.

Just as she said that the rope slipped and three men fell over backward, splash, into the lake!

"Now you see why they wear bathing suits, don't you, dear?" Mrs. Morton said, smiling.

After the tug of war came the races for the boys. Honey Bunch stood on tiptoe to watch the boat start, and as they came down the lake, she felt like cheering.

"Frankie has a blue stripe on his boat!" she told her daddy and mother. "See, there he is. Row, Frankie! Row!"

Frankie was rowing as hard as he could. His tongue stuck out of his mouth as it always did when he was working, and he was handling his oars the way his daddy had taught him. Frankie was also trying to keep cool, for that was another thing he had learned from his daddy.

"Don't get flustered," Mr. Evans had told him. "Keep your head."

Mr. Evans had been a famous oarsman

when he was in college, so he had always encouraged Frankie to row and had taught him how to manage a boat. Honey Bunch was so eager to have Frankie win the race that she felt as though she must do something to help him.

"Row, Frankie!" she called as loudly as she could. "You can win!"

Frankie heard her, and he put an extra spurt into the last yard. Another boat was very close to his, and Mr. Morton watched anxiously to see which went over the line first. The boat with the blue stripe shot in ahead.

"Frankie gets it!" Mr. Morton shouted, almost as excited as Honey Bunch.

He turned just in time to see Honey Bunch disappear over the side of the wharf and to hear a loud splash.

CHAPTER XIII

A NICE, QUIET NIGHT

"HONEY BUNCH!" cried Mrs. Morton. "Oh, David! Honey Bunch fell in!"

Mrs. Morton was going to jump into the water herself, after her little girl, when Honey Bunch stood up and tried to smile.

"I didn't mean to fall in," she said, her teeth chattering, for the water was cold. "I'm not hurt a bit, Mother! It's only up to me here!"

The water at the side of the wharf where Honey Bunch had stepped off, was only as high as her waist, but she had fallen in backward, and it was an uncomfortable surprise.

Her daddy had her out in a hurry. He wrapped his coat around her and carried her home. They did not stay to see the sham battle between the rafts which wound up Carnival Day. Mr. Morton built a fire, and

as soon as Honey Bunch had been rubbed dry
and popped into dry clothes, they had an
early supper. Then Honey Bunch was
drowsy—for the day had been full of excitement, and that does make a little girl tired—
and she went to sleep, but woke up when the
fireworks began.

"I do hope we'll have a nice, quiet night,"
said Mrs. Morton, as she was making up the
cots, after the last rocket had gone sailing up
into the sky and Labor Day was over for another year.

"Don't we always have quiet nights up here,
Mother?" Mr. Morton asked, covering the
fire.

"Yes, so far nothing has disturbed us," admitted Mrs. Morton. "But I think after a
day like this the young folks are apt to find it
difficult to settle down. They may go out
sailing on the lake and keep us awake with the
noise."

"I wouldn't want them to disturb Moonbeam Violet Leaf," Honey Bunch murmured
sleepily, as her mother tucked her into her

cot. "Fairies don't like noise, do they, Mother?"

Honey Bunch was asleep before her mother could answer her. She didn't know how long she had been asleep when something awoke her so suddenly she sat up in bed and began to cry.

"Mother!" she called. "Mother! What's the matter?"

Dear, dear, as soon as she said that there was a loud crash somewhere out in the darkness. Some one had fired a gun.

"Get him?" called a voice.

Honey Bunch scrambled out of her cot. She could see flashlights glowing from the different tents while lamps were lit in the bungalows and people began to shout across to each other.

"Mother!" cried Honey Bunch in terror. "Mother!"

Running feet sounded outside. Honey Bunch stumbled across to her mother's cot and put out her hands. The cot was empty!

Honey Bunch began to cry. She knew

something dreadful had happened. She turned to run to the tent door, tripped on her nightie, and the next thing she knew her mother held her safely in her arms.

"Were you frightened, darling?" asked Mrs. Morton, who had on her heavy dressing gown. "I went outside to see what all the fuss is about. There, you come into mother's bed and you'll be all right."

Honey Bunch cuddled down and tried to stop crying. She couldn't stop that minute, but she wasn't afraid any more.

"We're all safe and snug in our tent and daddy will come back and tell us what the trouble is soon," Mrs. Morton said, holding Honey Bunch close.

"Look at all the lights!" said Honey Bunch, the tears drying on her cheeks. "Every one is up, Mother. And you said you wanted a nice, quiet night."

Mrs. Morton laughed and pulled the blanket over Honey Bunch. A cool breeze was blowing in at the tent door.

"So I did! And this isn't exactly a quiet

night, is it, dear?" said Mrs. Morton. "I thought the first loud noise came from the boathouses. Go to sleep, dear. In the morning daddy will tell you everything that has happened."

Honey Bunch wanted to stay awake and hear that night, but, though she stared at a patch of light intently, it kept going farther and farther away. At last it got to be just a speck and finally it was gone entirely. Honey Bunch was fast asleep.

Every one in camp slept later than usual the next morning. They had worked hard on Carnival Day, and then to have so much excitement in the middle of the night—well, it was no wonder that breakfast was late in nearly every tent and bungalow.

Honey Bunch opened her eyes and sat up in bed to find her daddy and mother still asleep.

"I wonder if I could get dressed and surprise them?" she thought eagerly.

Her clothes were neatly folded on one of the camp chairs, for that was the way Honey Bunch had left them. Her clean blouse and tie were on top, and all she had to do was to take the little pile of garments out to the nearest "bathhouse" Larry Bert had built and dress there. Then, if she dropped a sandal, no one would hear the noise.

Honey Bunch could dress herself very neatly, though her mother sometimes had to help her with the buttons in hard places. But her khaki suit was easy to put on, and in a few minutes she was all ready.

She peeped in at the tent and saw that her mother and father were still sleeping.

"I could cook breakfast, I know I could," said Honey Bunch to herself. "But Mother won't let me light the stove."

Matches were one thing Honey Bunch was never allowed to touch.

"I'll take a walk," said Honey Bunch suddenly. "Mrs. Miller says a walk before breakfast is a tonic."

Honey Bunch did not look as though she needed any kind of tonic as she trotted off down the road that wound around the lake. Her blue eyes were dancing and her cheeks

were pink. A boy, coming up the road, waved
to her.

"It's Frankie Evans! Oh!" said Honey
Bunch.

She said, "oh" because she just remembered
what had happened the night before.

"Did you hear anything last night,
Frankie?" Honey Bunch called excitedly, before Frankie reached her.

"Hear anything!" replied Frankie. "Why,
I never heard such a racket in my life. I
couldn't go to sleep for a couple of hours. No
one could find out what it was all about till
your father discovered the roasting pan."

Honey Bunch looked astonished. What
could her daddy have to do with roasting
pans?

"Didn't you hear a noise?" asked Frankie.
"I don't see how you could sleep through all
that."

Honey Bunch explained that she hadn't
been asleep all the time.

"What was it?" she said, hopping up and

down in the road. "What was it, Frankie? Burglars?"

"Well, I'll tell you what it was," Frankie answered, delighted to have found some one to tell. "It was the three Hammer boys. They thought they saw a wildcat!"

"A wildcat?" repeated Honey Bunch. "The kind Norman Clark talks about?"

"I don't know anything about Norman Clark and his wildcat," Frankie said. "But Dick Hammer woke up last night and saw something big and dark outside their tent door. The three boys sleep together in a tent, you know.

"Dick has an air gun, and he thought this was his chance to shoot a wildcat. So he fired. But he couldn't see very well, and he hit the water pitcher and broke it."

"I heard him!" cried Honey Bunch. "Mother said it was a gun."

"That wasn't Dick's gun," Frankie explained a little impatiently. "That was Mr. Marshall's gun. He fired it off after Albert

Hammer went flying out of the tent crying that a burglar was in it."

"Then people lit their lights," said Honey Bunch, anxious to show that she had seen some of the excitement.

"Yes, they lit 'em, and there was the most awful crash out in the place where Mrs. Hammer keeps their food," Frankie went on. "It sounded like a million burglars, I guess. And my daddy got up and everybody got up and so did I. It was just like one time when a house on our block at home burned down—we got dressed and went to see it. But nobody could tell what made this noise."

"The roasting pan," said Honey Bunch comfortably.

"How did you know?" Frankie asked. "Oh, I said your father found it. Well, first Dick Hammer was sure he had seen a wildcat and my mother wanted my daddy to bring me in right away. But Dad said there were no wild animals up here. There aren't, either.

"So we went all through the trees and over the road and down to the boathouses and nobody could find anything. Then your father stepped on a roasting pan down by the wharf, and it had gravy in it. It was Mrs. Hammer's pan, and she said she had put it away with a pot roast in it."

"Did the wildcat take it?" said Honey Bunch, staring.

"I just told you there wasn't any wildcat," Frankie returned. "Dick had seen something all right; but it wasn't a wildcat. It was Rover, and he dragged that pan, with the meat in it, half way across the country. I'll bet he is hiding somewhere now. He always hides himself and sleeps after he has been stuffed like that."

"Oh, my!" said Honey Bunch. "And my mother wanted it to be a nice, quiet night."

"Well, it wasn't," Frankie declared. "I have to go get a loaf of bread. Want to come?"

"I'll go back and tell Mother I'm up," decided Honey Bunch. "She won't know where I went."

So Honey Bunch went back and found her

mother getting breakfast and wondering what
had become of her small daughter.

"I went for a walk for a tonic," said Honey
Bunch. "Were you surprised, Mother?"

"Yes, indeed," Mrs. Morton answered, kissing her. "So was Daddy. We were astonished not to find you in your cot when we
woke up."

"Frankie told me about the wildcat," said
Honey Bunch. "I think boys are funny; don't
you, Mother?"

"Sometimes," Mrs. Morton admitted.
"We'll hope the Hammer boys do not see another wildcat. And won't Norman be interested to hear what happened last night?"

"You like it here, don't you, Honey
Bunch?" her daddy asked her one night, as
they sat watching the campfire.

"Oh, yes," Honey Bunch answered. "But I
wish I could find Ida Grace. I keep thinking
perhaps Rose didn't get her after all, and she
may be somewhere in the bushes. Then if I
go home and leave her, she will freeze in the
winter."

"I wouldn't worry about Ida Grace," said Mr. Morton. "You see, Honey Bunch, if the little girl named Rose didn't find her—and she probably did—the fairies will take care of the dolly. They won't let her freeze. Moonbeam Violet Leaf will look after Ida Grace."

So Honey Bunch said she would try not to worry about her lost doll. But she was the least little bit lonely, in spite of the busy happy days she was spending.

"Wouldn't it be nice if Lady Clare was sitting in my lap, Mother?" she said once. "She would like the campfire. She likes to stare at the fireplace. I wonder if Lady Clare would like to see me?"

"Well, pretty soon she will see you, dear," replied Mrs. Morton. "We'll be going home soon, you know. But here comes Jennie Kirk and she looks as though she had something pleasant to tell us."

CHAPTER XIV

ANOTHER SURPRISE

JENNIE was out of breath, for she had been running. She usually did run, and her mother said she didn't see that she saved any time by hurrying so; she reached a place quickly, but it took her so long to get her breath back that she might as well have walked there slowly.

"Do—you—" gasped Jennie, as soon as she could speak. "Do—you want to—"

Honey Bunch gave a sudden bounce.

"Oh, yes, I do!" she cried. "Of course, I do, Jennie!"

That made every one laugh. Honey Bunch didn't know what Jennie was going to ask her, but she knew that Jennie always had something interesting to say. She liked the red-headed girl's plans.

Jennie sat down and fanned herself with a basket she carried. Of course a basket isn't a very good fan, but it is better than none.

"I wanted to ask you," said Jennie, "if you would like to go berry picking with us to-morrow. You know the second crop of black-berries is ripe. You have to hunt around some, but I know we can find enough for saucer pies. They're not as big as the first berries, but my mother says they are sweeter."

Honey Bunch did want to go blackberrying, and before she went to bed that night her mother had found a basket for her and she went to sleep holding it in her hand so that she would be ready bright and early the next morning.

Jennie had promised to come for her "right after breakfast," and she was on hand by half past seven, with Dora and Jessie and Frankie and Dick Hammer.

"We didn't tell the twins," said Jennie, "be-cause they can't walk very far and we'd have to bring them home before we had finished picking."

"Rover wanted to come," Frankie an-nounced. "So I let him."

Poor Rover had not been as popular at the

lake since he had hidden—or lost—Ida Grace and since he had taken Mrs. Hammer's pot roast, pan and all. But the children loved him just the same and, as Honey Bunch said, you couldn't expect a dog always to be good.

To reach the blackberry bushes, they had rather a long walk. It was a pleasant way, around the lake road, then through the pine grove, out into a wide stretch of sunny pastureland and then down a "back road" bordered on each side with the briary blackberry bushes.

"What are you going to do with your berries?" asked Dora Green as they tramped through the pine grove.

"Make saucer pies," returned Jennie promptly.

"I can make saucer pies," said Honey Bunch. "I made the loveliest saucer pie once, but Daddy sat on it. Are blackberry saucer pies good, Jennie?"

"'Licious," Jennie assured her. "You never tasted such good pie."

"Perhaps Mother will make me a saucer

pie," said Frankie. "But I like blackberry shortcake."

Jessie Waller giggled as she thought of something.

"Maybe we won't get any berries," she said. "Once my cousin was spending the summer on a farm and she was out driving and saw a huckleberry patch just loaded down with berries. And the next day she got every one on the farm and took the horse and wagon and all the pails and buckets she could find and drove to the patch and there wasn't a berry there!"

"Oh, my!" Honey Bunch cried in surprise. "What happened to 'em?"

"Some one had picked them, I suppose," said Jessie. "Perhaps all the blackberries will have been picked, too."

But when they came to the briary bushes on the back road, there were berries waiting for them. To be sure, the bushes were not loaded down, as they had been earlier in the season, but there were sweet ripe berries to be had for a little hunting. About every other berry went into the baskets and the others into little red mouths; but there is no fun in berrying unless you eat some. Any one will tell you that.

They picked until Dora declared that she had walked "miles and miles" and was tired.

"We have enough for saucer pies, anyway," she said. "There's nothing but green berries on this bush."

"Let's come again next week," Jennie suggested. "We're going home a week from Saturday, and it would be fun to pick more berries just before we have to go."

"All right, let's," agreed Dora. "Where are you going, Honey Bunch?"

"I saw a flower," Honey Bunch returned. "I want to save it for my collection."

Honey Bunch had two collections of which she was very proud. Her daddy was helping her make them. One was a collection of the leaves of the different trees, pressed in a book, and the other collection was of wild flowers. Honey Bunch meant to give the wild flower collection to Mrs. Lancaster, the old lady who had given her the seeds from which she had raised her prize-winning flowers.

"Let's all pick flowers for Honey Bunch," suggested Dora, forgetting that she was tired. "Come on, I see lots of them."

They left Rover to guard their baskets of berries and went further down the road, picking the late wild flowers that were blooming in the tangle of weeds and grasses that bordered the fields. Picking flowers reminded Honey Bunch of the two little girls, Jane and Sarah, who had sold wild flowers along the shore road. She told Jennie and Dora and the others about them, and Jennie said that Honey Bunch always had something interesting happening to her.

"Nothing ever happens to me," sighed Jennie.

Just as she said that the fence against which she was leaning—and which was old and worm-eaten—broke. Over went Jennie into a brush heap. There might have been anything in that brush heap, from snakes to baby rabbits, and it was certainly a prickly place to tumble, for the old dead twigs and roots scratched Jennie on her face and arms as she struggled to get up.

"I'll help you," cried Frankie, and he and Dick Hammer rushed over to pull Jennie out.

Jennie was an outdoor girl, and she didn't mind a tumble now and then. She could take care of herself in the water, and she wasn't afraid of anything on land, except one thing. Just one thing! A spider frightened her dreadfully. Even little tiny spiders that could not possibly hurt any one.

"There's a spider—ow!" shrieked Jennie, as she reached up her hands to Frankie who was ready to pull her to her feet.

A small black spider was running down the sleeve of Jennie's dress. She knocked it off with such force that she smashed it, and then she scrambled to her feet without any help and ran. She ran down the road as though an army of spiders was chasing her.

No one wanted to laugh, because Jennie was so serious. But Honey Bunch looked at Dora and Dora looked at Frankie and Dick said something about "she said nothing ever happens to her," and then they began to snicker. In another minute they were laughing so hard that Frankie choked and Dick was almost crying.

"I don't see anything funny," poor Jennie said, when she came back, warm and tired from her run down the road.

"You said nothing ever happens to you," Frankie reminded her, and that made them all laugh again. Even Jennie had to laugh, too.

It was time now to start home, and each took his or her berry basket and woke up Rover, who may have been a good watch dog, but who liked to take a nap pretty often. They didn't see a single spider on the way home, and if you can not guess what they had for their suppers that night, I will tell. Blackberry saucer pie!

"Honey Bunch," said Mrs. Morton, a few mornings later, "Daddy is going down to Barham. The office sent for him, and he will have to stay one night, at least. You and I will stay with Mrs. Applegate while he's away."

"Will he see Lady Clare?" asked Honey
Bunch eagerly.

"I think he'll go to Mrs. Miller's," Mrs.
Morton answered. "And he can take a message to Lady Clare if you like."

So when Mr. Morton was ready to go to the
station, Honey Bunch stood up on the trunk
and whispered in his ear:

"Tell Lady Clare," she whispered, "that I
love her more than ever and I miss her very
much. Tell her I hope she is having a good
time. And tell her that Ida Grace is lost.
Please, Daddy—thank you."

Mr. Morton promised to give Lady Clare
the message, and then he hurried off to catch
his train. Camp Snapdragon seemed lonely
without him, and Honey Bunch and her
mother were glad when Mrs. Napoleon came
for them with her launch and took them for a
long sail and a picnic lunch on the little island
at the top of the lake. Mrs. Hendricks and
Charles Augustus were there, too, and Honey
Bunch was surprised to find that the baby had
grown.

"Do they grow a little every day, or all at once—babies, I mean?" she asked Mrs. Hendricks.

"I think they grow a little every day," Mrs. Hendricks replied. "Think how big Charles Augustus will be when you see him next year, Honey Bunch."

For every one at Lake Tickaloc planned to come back the next summer. They planned what they would do and some of them even had their floats designed for the next Carnival Day. Honey Bunch hoped she and daddy and mother would come again, and Frankie and Dora and Jessie and Jennie and the Hammer boys all said they wanted to spend another summer in camp.

That night Honey Bunch and her mother stayed at the bungalow with Mrs. Applegate, and that dear woman seemed to think they had had nothing to eat since the last time they had visited her. She kept asking them to eat more, and when she had to put away a large layer cake that had not even been cut, she felt very bad.

"But you can take it with you to-morrow," she said. "Mr. Morton will be coming home, and he likes layer cake."

And in the morning when Honey Bunch and her mother went back to their camp so as to be ready when Daddy Morton came, Mrs. Applegate had a basket packed for them, and there were many good things to eat in it besides the chocolate layer cake.

"When will Daddy come, Mother?" Honey Bunch kept asking. "I wonder if he saw Lady Clare? Maybe she wasn't at home when he went to see Mrs. Miller. Sometimes Lady Clare takes a long walk, and she doesn't come back till dark."

"I'm wondering if Daddy went to our house," said Mrs. Morton. "I'd like to know if everything is all right there. Whether the man came to cut the grass as he promised and whether Mrs. Farriday has kept the flowers picked in our garden."

Mrs. Farriday had promised to pick the flowers that blossomed and to give them to people who had no flower gardens.

"I see Daddy!" shouted Honey Bunch at
last, when she had been watching the road for
an hour that afternoon. "Here he comes!
And, oh, Mother, he has a basket! Maybe he
went picking blackberries."

But Mr. Morton had not been berrying.
He said so when Honey Bunch flew out to
meet him and asked him.

"That basket is for you," he declared, giving
her a kiss. "Open it with care, Honey Bunch."

Honey Bunch lifted the lid and peeped in.
Then she began to hop up and down and to
laugh with delight.

"Daddy! Daddy! Daddy!" she cried.
"Oh, Mother, come quick and look!"

CHAPTER XV

WHAT HONEY BUNCH FOUND

HONEY BUNCH was so excited she couldn't keep still. She danced around the table and hugged the basket and then rushed at Daddy Morton and hugged him, too.

"It's Lady Clare!" she exclaimed over and over. "My darling Lady Clare! My own dear kitty cat! Where did you find her, Daddy?"

"At Mrs. Miller's," Daddy Morton explained, smiling. "I thought a little camp life would be good for kitty, so I brought her along."

Mrs. Morton had to take Lady Clare out of the basket and smooth her ruffled fur, for Honey Bunch could only dance around and sing. Cats do not like to travel, and Lady Clare was inclined to be a little cross; but when she found she was among her friends, she felt better at once and sat down on the floor and began to lick her fur.

Honey Bunch had not known how much she missed Lady Clare until she saw her again. And the cat seemed very glad to be with her little mistress. She followed Honey Bunch everywhere she went, sat watching the camp-fire with her, and took walks with her down the road. The other children thought she was a beautiful cat—as indeed she was—and Lady Clare had so much attention paid to her that it is a wonder it did not make her vain.

"I never saw a cat in camp before," said Jennie Kirk one morning, not long after Lady Clare arrived. "But I do believe she likes it."

"Of course she does," Honey Bunch declared. "She sleeps all night on a piece of blanket beside the fire—Daddy says it doesn't get cold till 'most morning. And she likes to sit on the wharf and watch the water. I think she is watching the baby fish. She has a good time."

"Aren't you afraid she will catch the

fairy?" asked Jennie anxiously. "She might think she was a bird or something."

"I guess Lady Clare knows a fairy when she sees one!" Honey Bunch replied indignantly. "Anyway, she doesn't catch birds—hardly ever. Lady Clare is a brought-up cat. My mother brought her up."

"Well, perhaps she doesn't eat fairies then," admitted Jennie. "I just wasn't sure."

That afternoon Honey Bunch and Lady Clare were keeping house all alone. Mr. and Mrs. Morton had gone for a row and Honey Bunch was waiting for Dora and Jennie to stop for her on their way to the post-office. Lady Clare sat beside her on an old log and Honey Bunch was stroking her fur when the cat began to growl—little, low rumbling growls the way a thunderstorm sounds when it is beginning.

"What's the matter?" asked Honey Bunch, surprised.

Lady Clare rose to her feet, her back arching, her tail all fluffed out. She began to spit furiously. She was staring up the road, and

when Honey Bunch looked, she understood.
There was Rover coming toward them.

"Go away!" called Honey Bunch. "Go
away, Rover! You scare Lady Clare."

Rover was a kind-hearted dog, and as a rule
he did whatever was asked of him. But he
was a bow-wow and he simply could not pass
a kitty-cat by. No, sir, he had to chase them!
Dogs are like that. He paid no attention to
Honey Bunch, but ran directly toward Lady
Clare, who gave one last awful spit and turned
and fled.

Fortunately, there were plenty of trees close
at hand, and Lady Clare knew what to do.
Up a tall, straight young oak tree ran the cat,
and she never stopped till she was almost at
the top. Then she looked down and glared at
Rover, who was barking furiously.

Frankie, coming up the road a few minutes
later, found Honey Bunch crying and Rover
still barking at the cat.

"Lady Clare will never come down," sobbed
Honey Bunch. "When she gets up so high,

she is afraid to come down. She'll be lost the
way Ida Grace was."

"No, she won't," Frankie said stoutly.
"You can't lose a cat. I'll take Rover home
and tie him up, and then I'll get Lady Clare
down for you."

But when Frankie came back after tying
Rover, he found that it was not so easy as he
had thought to get the cat down. She kept
going higher and higher and she mewed as
though she were frightened.

"Once a cat at home stayed in a tree all night
and kept us awake by crying," said Frankie,
who tried to climb the tree and found it more
than he could do.

"I don't want her to stay in the tree all
night," Honey Bunch protested.

"Well, if she had more sense, she'd come
down herself," said Frankie. "You would
think she'd know better than to keep climbing
up. Why doesn't she climb down?"

But Lady Clare kept climbing higher till
she was at the very top of the tree. She was
afraid to come down, and you know yourself,

if you climb trees, that it is easier to go up
than to come down. Of course you can fall
down, but not even a cat wishes to fall down
a tree.

"How did the cat get down—the one that
stayed in the tree all night?" asked Honey
Bunch, staring up in the tree at Lady Clare.

"Oh, the firemen came with ladders and
took her down," Frankie said.

"Are there any firemen up here?" demanded
Honey Bunch, and when Frankie said no, she
was disappointed.

"Larry Bert has a ladder!" she said suddenly. "He'll get Lady Clare down. Come
on, Frankie, let's go ask him."

Dora and Jennie saw them running and ran
after them. When they heard about Lady
Clare they were sorry for her, and Jennie was
sure that Larry would have a long ladder,
long enough to reach to the top of the tree.

"Can I get a cat out of a tree?" said Larry,
when he heard the story. "Well, now, I might
try. I used to be a sailor, and I can climb.
Show me this tree and this cat, Honey Bunch."

He didn't take a ladder with him, but he didn't need one. They came to the tree and found Lady Clare mewing louder than ever at the very tiptop. The children watched Larry climb the tree. He did it very easily, and it was exciting to watch him working his way up. Poor Lady Clare was more frightened than ever when she saw him coming, and if there had been a higher branch to climb to, she would have climbed out on it. She was up as high as she could go, however; so all she could do was to dig her claws in and hold tight and spit at Larry when he put out his hand to lift her down.

"She'll scratch him!" cried Frankie, whose neck was beginning to hurt from bending it, he said.

But Lady Clare didn't scratch Larry. He didn't give her a chance. He picked her off that branch as though she had been a banana or a coconut, and almost before she knew what was happening to her, she found herself on the ground.

"And when she calms down, she'll find she

has all her nine lives still," said Larry cheerfully. "Any one else need to be rescued to-
day, Honey Bunch?"

Honey Bunch thought not and said "thank
you" to Larry, who replied that he liked to
go after cats.

"Now, a dog is too much work," he told
her. "When I see a dog up in a tree I'm apt
to let him stay there. They're so heavy to
carry."

"He's fooling us," Frankie said, when Larry
had gone whistling back to his storehouse.
"Dogs don't climb trees."

Lady Clare was all right again as soon as
she had smoothed her fur and had a nap, and
in a few days she was so used to Rover that
she would not run when she saw him coming.
Before Lady Clare went back to Barham, she
and the dog were the best of friends—that is,
as good friends as a bow-wow and a kitty-cat
ever are.

But another adventure was waiting for
Honey Bunch before she and Lady Clare went
home. Of course she did not know an ad-

venture was around the corner the morning
she and the other children started for their
last berry-picking party. It was Thursday,
and on Saturday Honey Bunch and Jennie
and Dora were going home. Frankie and the
Hammer boys were going the following week,
and Saunders Abbott and Jessie Waller had
already gone. It was almost the end of the
season at Lake Tickaloc.

"Let's go on the other side of the road this
time," suggested Jennie, as they walked along
with their baskets. "We saw a lot of green
berries there. Remember? The sun's been so
hot they may have dried up, but perhaps they
will be ripe. You never can tell."

The other children were willing to pick
anywhere they were asked to. They thought
they were more interested in the walk than in
the berries. But when they came to the back
road and found more berries ripe than the
week before, they all set to work with a will,
saucer pies floating through each mind.

"Here's a good bush," called Honey Bunch,
and she tried to part a scraggly bush to get at

the berries she could see behind a screen of dead wood and briars.

Then a squeal of surprise and delight startled the other children.

"I've found her!" Honey Bunch shrieked. "Dora! Jennie! I've found Ida Grace! And she isn't hurt a bit!"

My goodness, no one thought of blackberries after that. There was the lost Ida Grace, as smiling as when they had last seen her. There were a few stains on her khaki blouse and her tie had faded, but, aside from that, she was as good as ever. She had not been rained on, and whatever Rover had done to her, he had not hurt her in any way.

"He hid her under a porch or somewhere, during that storm, and then he brought her out here and left her," insisted Frankie. "I'll bet she has been here ever since."

Ida Grace could not talk and tell her experiences, but Honey Bunch did not mind, now that she had found her. The children picked a few more berries, and then went home with the good news. Mrs. Morton declared

that Honey Bunch should give a party for Ida
Grace, and the very next night the children
gathered around the fire at Camp Snapdragon
and Ida Grace wore the blue sweater Mrs.
Hendricks had made for her.

It was a lovely party, for they sang songs
and each one had to tell a story. Mr. Morton
gave each one a small stick of wood to put on
the fire, and as long as that burned, the one
who had put the stick on must tell a story.
Some of the stories were funny, and Frankie
made them laugh because he was so interested
in watching his stick burn through that he forgot to talk.

After the stories they had ice-cream and
cake—and you may be sure Mrs. Applegate
made the cake, and very good it was—and then
lollipops.

"We're going home to-morrow," said Honey
Bunch, staring at the dancing flames which
were winking at her.

"So are we," said Dora and Jennie together,
and then they laughed for they sounded just
like the Foster twins.

Benny and Bertha were blinking. They had been invited to the party, and perhaps no one at the lake was as glad as little Bertha that Ida Grace had been found. She had really lost her, you see, and no one wants to lose a friend's doll.

"I have to go back to school next week," Frankie announced importantly. "I have to study ever so hard this year."

The three Hammer boys were going back to school, too.

"I like to go home," declared Honey Bunch. "I'll see Mrs. Miller and Mrs. Farriday and Mrs. Lancaster and Ida Camp and, oh, everybody."

"It's always nice to go home," Jennie said. "And I'll see you next year, Honey Bunch."

That was what every one was saying the next morning. A great many people were going home on the afternoon train, and Larry Bert was busy helping them close their camps and taking the furniture back to the storehouse. He would take down the tents later when he had more time.

"See you next year!" people called cheerfully to each other, as they said good-by. "Don't forget—see you next year!"

When the Mortons were almost ready to go, Honey Bunch took Lady Clare under one arm and Ida Grace under the other and went down to the wharf. She stood there all alone and looked at the water.

"Good-by, Lake Tickaloc," she said softly. "Good-by, Camp Snapdragon. I've had a lovely time!"

Then her daddy called to her to hurry or they would miss the train. For the happy summer was over for Honey Bunch and Ida Grace and Lady Clare. It was time to go home.

THE END

THE HONEY BUNCH BOOKS

By HELEN LOUISE THORNDYKE

Individual Colored Wrappers and Text Illustrations

Honey Bunch is a dainty, thoughtful little girl, and to know her is to take her to your heart at once.

Little girls everywhere will want to discover what interesting experiences she is having wherever she goes.

HONEY BUNCH: JUST A LITTLE GIRL
HONEY BUNCH: HER FIRST VISIT TO THE CITY
HONEY BUNCH: HER FIRST DAYS ON THE FARM
HONEY BUNCH: HER FIRST VISIT TO THE SEASHORE
HONEY BUNCH: HER FIRST LITTLE GARDEN
HONEY BUNCH: HER FIRST DAYS IN CAMP
HONEY BUNCH: HER FIRST AUTO TOUR
HONEY BUNCH: HER FIRST TRIP ON THE OCEAN
HONEY BUNCH: HER FIRST TRIP WEST
HONEY BUNCH: HER FIRST SUMMER ON AN ISLAND
HONEY BUNCH: HER FIRST TRIP ON THE GREAT LAKES
HONEY BUNCH: HER FIRST TRIP IN AN AEROPLANE
HONEY BUNCH: HER FIRST VISIT TO THE ZOO
HONEY BUNCH: HER FIRST BIG ADVENTURE
HONEY BUNCH: HER FIRST BIG PARADE
HONEY BUNCH: HER FIRST LITTLE MYSTERY
HONEY BUNCH: HER FIRST LITTLE CIRCUS
HONEY BUNCH: HER FIRST LITTLE TREASURE HUNT

GROSSET & DUNLAP   :-:   *Publishers*   :-:   NEW YORK

The MARY and JERRY MYSTERY STORIES
By FRANCIS HUNT

THE MESSENGER DOG'S SECRET

The big police dog Flanders carried a strange message in his collar. By following its directions, Mary and Jerry Denton were able to bring a lost fortune to someone in need.

THE MYSTERY OF THE TOY BANK

Jerry Denton was saving for a bicycle, but when his little bank strangely disappeared he had a big mystery to solve. With the aid of Mary, several chums and a queer old sailor, this eager lad brought about a happy solution.

THE STORY THE PARROT TOLD

A fire in a pet shop started a long chain of adventures for Mary and Jerry Denton. The tale the talking parrot told caused plenty of excitement and mystery before the bird was restored to its rightful owner.

THE SECRET OF THE MISSING CLOWN

Mary and Jerry have many happy adventures at the circus while searching for the missing clown and his beautiful pony, Silverfeet.

GROSSET & DUNLAP   *Publishers*   NEW YORK

Three Stories of Fun and Friendship

THE MAIDA BOOKS
by INEZ HAYNES IRWIN

MAIDA'S LITTLE SHOP

In a darling little shop of her own Maida makes many friends with the school children who buy her fascinating wares.

MAIDA'S LITTLE HOUSE

All of her friends spend a happy summer in Maida's perfect little house that has everything a child could wish for.

MAIDA'S LITTLE SCHOOL

Three delightful grownups come to visit and the children study many subjects without knowing that they are really "going to school."

GROSSET & DUNLAP   *Publishers*   NEW YORK

THE BOBBSEY TWINS BOOKS
FOR LITTLE MEN AND WOMEN
By LAURA LEE HOPE

ILLUSTRATED. *Every volume complete in itself.*

These books for boys and girls between the ages of three and ten stand among children and their parents of this generation where the books of Louisa May Alcott stood in former days. The haps and mishaps of this inimitable pair of twins, their many adventures and experiences are a source of keen delight to imaginative children.

THE BOBBSEY TWINS
THE BOBBSEY TWINS IN THE COUNTRY
THE BOBBSEY TWINS AT THE SEASHORE
THE BOBBSEY TWINS AT SCHOOL
THE BOBBSEY TWINS AT SNOW LODGE
THE BOBBSEY TWINS ON A HOUSEBOAT
THE BOBBSEY TWINS AT MEADOW BROOK
THE BOBBSEY TWINS AT HOME
THE BOBBSEY TWINS IN A GREAT CITY
THE BOBBSEY TWINS ON BLUEBERRY ISLAND
THE BOBBSEY TWINS ON THE DEEP BLUE SEA
THE BOBBSEY TWINS IN WASHINGTON
THE BOBBSEY TWINS IN THE GREAT WEST
THE BOBBSEY TWINS AT CEDAR CAMP
THE BOBBSEY TWINS AT THE COUNTY FAIR
THE BOBBSEY TWINS CAMPING OUT
THE BOBBSEY TWINS AND BABY MAY
THE BOBBSEY TWINS KEEPING HOUSE
THE BOBBSEY TWINS AT CLOVERBANK
THE BOBBSEY TWINS AT CHERRY CORNER
THE BOBBSEY TWINS AND THEIR SCHOOLMATES
THE BOBBSEY TWINS TREASURE HUNTING
THE BOBBSEY TWINS AT SPRUCE LAKE
THE BOBBSEY TWINS WONDERFUL SECRET
THE BOBBSEY TWINS AT THE CIRCUS
THE BOBBSEY TWINS ON AN AIRPLANE TRIP
THE BOBBSEY TWINS SOLVE A MYSTERY
THE BOBBSEY TWINS ON A RANCH
THE BOBBSEY TWINS IN ESKIMO LAND

GROSSET & DUNLAP :-: *Publishers* :-: NEW YORK